THE CARVINGS

OF COBBEMARMOO

The Second Book

Of Dubious Magic

For my darling bride

and for those who might see themselves in here, and smile.

I'd like to thank my supporters at www.patreon.com/Renoir

- with special thanks to Tegan McKechnie.

Published by ***Meredian Pictures & Words 2016***
Angels Beach, Australia

CONTENTS

1 FIRST SITE

There are a lot of things that many white people don't like about the Australian desert. People of other colours probably don't like those things either, but the white ones seem to complain more. The heat. The glare. The feelings of emptiness and isolation. The fifty million blowflies.

The three archaeologists walking away from the dusty four-wheel-drive truck were oblivious to all of the above. The men sweated as they walked through a landscape tinted in all shades of red and ochre. Up an incline they picked their way, through scattered rocks interlaced with the coarse sand that swept as far as the eye could see in any direction.

The white shirt and khaki shorts of one of the men showed less grime, sweat and flyblow than his companions, indicating that he was a new arrival. The grizzled older man leading the single file addressed the newcomer and inclined his head.

"I asked Mr. Drayden to, park a little way away so you might get a sense of the, conditions in which we, are working. Over here," he said.

Initially hidden by the ridge of a small depression were two neat tents, a table, chairs and several boxes under a canvas fly. Nearby, bright orange tape edged a rectangle about a metre and a half wide that extended from the front of a sandstone ledge perhaps three metres long. Outside the taped area were numerous piles of sand, obviously heaped up deliberately, not by the wind. The big clue would be the shovel protruding from one pile.

The man in the clean white shirt stepped over the tape and peered into the space that had been cleared under the ledge. He took a small torch from his pocket and shone the beam across the underside of the stone shelf. Beneath it had been cleared of sand only to a depth of just over a metre, but the space reached back a surprising distance. He stroked his short beard as his eyes followed the torchlight.

"Fascinating," he said, his soft American voice scarcely audible to the other two men, standing behind him with their arms folded.

After a few moments inspection he poked his head out from under the ledge and said, "You've done remarkably well to find this, Professor Bevan."

The older man nodded graciously and replied, "My first intimation came, from a European colleague visiting our University. Professor Krieg mentioned to me some obscure suggestions of, a Mediterranean connection with Central, Australia. I came out here to, investigate. The carvings, on the lip of the rock were first described, later shown to me by a native. I sensed, there was more to them than met the eye so I enlisted, the aid of young Drayden here." The professor's voice was wheezy, and he had a disconcerting manner of punctuating his speech with oddly timed brief pauses. "Age has wearied me, somewhat, I'm afraid, so far as heavy labour is concerned, and Drayden, is very fit, as well as having been one of, my better students."

The lean, weathered features of Drayden showed no acknowledgement of his mentor's faint praise. There was an air of suppressed tension about him.

"A native?" enquired the American. "You mean one of the local tribes people? Do they live nearby?"

Drayden frowned sourly. "Nobody lives nearby here…"

The older man cut him off. "Whatever nomadic tribes, may have once frequented, this area are long gone. There are a handful of small, groups scattered among these ranges, but none have shown any, particular interest in, or knowledge of, this site. There are many other, Aboriginals now making their homes, in the city to our south. Quite urbanized, in their way. It was from one such fellow – in a bar I must admit – that I first heard of, this spot. I presume him to be some sort, of distant descendant. The tradition of oral history still has some, currency among the 'town' Aboriginals, even if few other traditions do."

The American may have frowned slightly at the professor's dismissive tone.

"There are more like this, you say?" he enquired.

"Similar, but quite, distinct. Some way from here, I'm afraid. We'll drive there next. I had it in mind, for you to look after the, other location while Drayden and I continued here. But I would value your, thoughts on what you see before you."

Drayden's deeply tanned face darkened further. The American gave no sign of noticing as he said, "I'd like to make some sketches…"

"Later, I'm sure," interrupted Bevan. "I'd like to be setting off for, Location Number Two, so Drayden and I can be back, here before dark. We only have the other site, set up to accommodate one person, you see."

At a nod from the professor, Drayden ducked under the overhang, grasped the newcomer's arm and firmly guided him back into the sunlight.

"Ah, well – if you're quite sure…"

"Yes. I only stopped, here because it was en route, as it were, and to give you some context. I would prefer your, focus to be the material at Location Number Two."

As the three men climbed back into the vehicle there was a short beep from the professor's wristwatch.

The newcomer glanced at his own watch then smiled as he said, "Ah – chimes on the quarter hour. There's something charmingly old-fashioned about that."

"Thank you," acknowledged Bevan politely. "Consider this, gentlemen…"

Drayden rolled his eyes. He was all too familiar with the professor's 'little intellectual challenges' that he always prefaced with those words.

The older man continued, "If you were unable to, actually see my watch and heard it emit, a single beep, what is the longest period of time you'd have to, wait before being sure of the correct time?"

"An hour – no – forty five minutes," said Drayden.

The American looked thoughtful and mused, "That seems too obvious…"

Bevan nodded. "Indeed, sir. Between 12:15 and 1:45 you would hear seven single tones, and know that the next time must be two o'clock."

"So the answer is ninety minutes. Very clever, professor," said the new arrival.

Bevan smiled smugly.

The scowl on Drayden's face darkened a little further. "Don't encourage him," he muttered.

As Drayden continued to drive the vehicle across the scorching terrain, Bevan looked over his glasses at the American. "Your thoughts, on Location 1?" he asked.

"As I said – fascinating. If I'd seen them as photographs, with no clue as to their location, I'd still have been impressed. But to find them here… if they're genuine, this will upset a lot of widely accepted theory."

"Indeed. My very thought," said the professor.

In truth, if he were to share them Bevan's very thoughts would have upset a great deal more than accepted theory.

There should have been a roll of portentous thunder. There was only the roar of the motor, and the drone of the flies.

.o0o.

2 PICKING UP THE STORY

"Hitch hiker ahead," said a voice from the back seat of the Triumph sedan as it cruised up the highway towards the centre of Australia.

"Yeah. So?" replied the driver.

"Aw c'mon Wilko. You can't leave the poor bugger at the side of the road out here in the middle of nowhere." The voice belonged to John B. Stewart: public servant, Scotch drinker, currently holiday-maker, and possibly a quite powerful wizard. Not everyone was convinced of the latter, and John B. himself was more than a little vague about exactly what his power was and how it worked.

"Sure can. This is Highway One, John, even if it doesn't look much like it. There'll be plenty of other cars and trucks along. There's already four of us and a cat in here – we couldn't fit anyone else in."

 Robert 'Wilko' Wilkes was one of the people least convinced of John B.'s magical powers, although he was at a loss to explain the bizarre coincidences that seemed to keep happening in the presence of his shaggy-haired mate.

"Fair go, mate. It must be over 40 degrees out there. We're only a couple of hours out of Alice Springs. Scarlet and I can make a bit of room back here…"

 'Scarlet' – real name Charlotte O'Hara Burke – gave her companion in the back seat a frosty glare and said, "Can we, indeed? I don't suppose the fact that she's blonde and obviously female has anything to do with your generosity of spirit."

"Scarlet, how could you think that of me? You know I'd never look at another woman when you're around."

"That's not funny, John," was Scarlet's cold reply.

"Well, no, I suppose not. Nor true, either," conceded John B. "Come on, Wilko. Look at her. Poor thing's probably sunburned half to death."

The Triumph stopped, and began to slowly reverse back towards the rather surprised hitch hiker.

The current occupant of the front passenger seat was John B.'s housemate back in Canberra, a tall thin young man named Darren Bond. He leaned back over his seat and asked "Psst, John – why didn't you just wish Wilko to stop?"

Stewart shook his head. "Magic's serious stuff, man. I can't just abuse it, y'know. Besides, I figured that we could rely on Wilko's chivalrous nature. And the fact I know he's got a weakness for blondes, too." Both Scarlet and Wilko snorted in response, although perhaps for different reasons.

As the car stopped a rear passenger door opened and John B. stepped gallantly out. The blonde hitch-hiker was confronted by a long haired, slightly overweight figure in jeans and a purple t-shirt. His left hand was swathed in bandages like a badly drawn cartoon mummy.

John B. gave a smile that he hoped looked warm, sincere and alluring. He was completely wrong, but he did at least look harmless. "Like a lift?" he asked.

"No thanks. I'm standing out here practising to become a solar battery."

"Ah. Nice to have a hobby. Where are you headed?"

"Up past Alice Springs, into the McDonnell Ranges. But Alice itself would do nicely if you could manage."

"We can do that much, at least," Stewart assured her.

"Um, are you sure there's room?" the girl asked uncertainly.

"Yeah, no problem. We'll squeeze your pack into the boot." He called to the driver, "Wilko, can I have the keys please mate?"

As he opened the boot he introduced himself and held out his good hand. The girl shook it and smiled broadly. "Jazz," she said.

"Sorry?"

"Jazz. That's my name."

"Oh, right. That's cool. Come on, Kat, shift over."

Jazz was a little disconcerted to see a large white Persian cat in the boot of the Triumph. At John B.'s prodding he moved rather grumpily to one side to allow the pack to be squeezed in to the capacious luggage space.

"Is he alright in there?" she asked uncertainly.

"Oh yeah," John B. reassured her. "If he gets bored he sneaks through the gap under the back seat and joins us."

"Uh-huh…" Jazz replied, unconvinced. Kat didn't look like he could squeeze through any gap much smaller than a manhole.

"Come on, Jazz. It's cooking out here."

Squeezed snugly into the Triumph, Jazz introduced herself. "It's actually Jacinta – Jacinta Parrish. But that was my Mum's name for me, and I never liked it much. Pop always calls me Jazz, and that's who I am." In turn, she was introduced to her new travelling companions: Darren - pizza cook, weapons collector and fantasy war games enthusiast; Scarlet – computer analyst and keen student of the occult; and Wilko - the owner and driver of the Triumph, who worked with Scarlet and John B. and openly considered himself the only normal one of the four.

"So what do you do?" Jazz asked John B.

"I'm a wizard."

"Oh wow! Really?"

John B. blinked in some surprise. Scarlet and Darren had hitherto been the only people who actually believed him when he said that, and in Scarlet's case it was only after she carried out her own surreptitious tests to satisfy her skepticism.

He proceeded to tell Jazz the story of how he'd struck his head on a poker machine (neglecting to mention that he was extremely drunk at the time), and how ever since then every time he wished for something, it happened.

Jazz looked a little bemused. "It doesn't sound like any of the other wizards I've ever met," she said.

Scarlet looked suspicious. She was ever alert for practitioners of what she called The Black Arts, and recent experience had given an edge to her usual caution. "What part of England are you from, Jazz? I've been trying to pick your accent."

"Well, originally, from Stratford-upon-Avon. But I've travelled around a lot."

"Meeting wizards?" Scarlet sounded something more than careful.

"People who claimed to be, at least. A couple in Glastonbury, back home. And some really interesting guys in Ghana. They all relied on casting actual spells and sacrifices and such, though."

"Bunch of crap," observed Wilko.

"But what about…?" Darren began to protest.

"What about nothing!" Wilko cut him off. "John's got a drunk's gift for weird coincidences, that's all."

Jazz decided a change of subject might be diplomatic. "I noticed the Canberra number plate. What are you guys doing up this way, anyhow? On holidays?"

It didn't seem appropriate to explain that they'd originally come to outback Australia to find the people who'd been trying to kill John B., and had found themselves battling a mad sorceress and an other-dimensional demon in a cavern underneath a secret US satellite tracking station. Having barely escaped with their lives they had decided to head north for what they considered was a well-earned rest.

"Yeah. Holidays. That's it," agreed John B.

"What did you do to your hand?"

"Er… I hit it on something and broke it."

Again, it didn't seem a good idea to go into details, given that the 'something' was the jaw of a US army colonel who had been about to shoot them. Or that the colonel had subsequently had his brain turned into cabbage, and been buried when the demon was defeated and the underground cavern collapsed.

"That was careless," Jazz observed, solicitously.

"I think I was drunk," admitted John B.

It was Scarlet's turn to decide that a change of subject was in order. "What were you doing in Ghana, Jazz?" she asked.

"Helping build a bridge. I'm an engineer. I travel a lot looking for work."

Wilko's eyebrows rose as he looked again at their new passenger in his rear view mirror. 'Definitely not the usual image of an engineer', he thought to himself. "Is that why you're off to the Alice?" he asked.

"No, I'm going to meet my boyfriend."

Both Wilko and John B. deflated almost visibly.

"He's an archaeologist," Jazz continued, "working in the ranges up north of the centre. A tiny little place called Cobbemarmoo."

Darren consulted their map. "I don't see it," he said.

"I don't know that there's anything much there," the blonde engineer explained. "Harlan says that's the aboriginal name for the place. I gather it's not much more than a collection of rocks."

*

"We'll be in Alice soon," Wilko advised. "Where can we drop you?"

"At the Post Office, please. Harlan said he'd leave a message for me there telling me how to find him. After I've checked there, can I buy you guys a drink to say 'thanks' for the lift?"

"What a wonderful idea," enthused John B.

Scarlet raised an eyebrow at him. "I thought you were going to get to a doctor and have that hand set properly?"

"How long can that take? We can meet up somewhere afterwards. We've got to find a place to stay, anyhow."

In fact, things worked out quite smoothly. Jazz was dropped at the Post Office, John B. was able to get straight in to see the obliging, capable (and not at all awkwardly curious) Dr. Margaret Jones almost next door, and the others didn't have to drive far to find a big old house with rooms to rent and no objections to Kat's presence.

*

Little more than an hour after arriving in Alice Springs the group was reassembled in a large airy tavern overlooking the waterless Todd River. Wilko was looking concerned as he spoke to Jazz.

"No message at all? That doesn't help much! Is he usually – er – reliable?"

"Oh yeah. Well, pretty much. In a kind of vague, academic way. He might leave a message that wasn't much bloody use to me, but he wouldn't forget me completely. I just hope he's okay."

"He doesn't have a mobile phone with him?" asked Wilko.

 Jazz shook her head. "Nah – he never bothers with them. Me neither."

"You too? None of this bunch believe in them either!" the Tasmanian complained.

 With a shrug Jazz explained, "We both travel too much for any of the networks or plans to be much use."

"I get that," agreed Wilko. "I've read what they charge for International Roaming."

"And even if the rates were okay, Harlan and I are both too often in places where the coverage is lousy or non-existent."

"So what will you do now?" asked Scarlet.

"Wait, I guess. His expedition will have to come back into town for supplies sooner or later."

 Wilko looked slightly relieved. "So there is a whole expedition of them, is there?"

Jazz shrugged. "It's supposed to be a University-run dig, so I'd assume there'd be at least a couple of people on it doing different jobs. It's not just him, at any rate. No point in worrying just yet, I suppose. Maybe I got here earlier than he expected, or maybe whatever he's working on is just really, really interesting."

There was no bitterness or suspicion in her voice. There was no reason for anyone at the table to guess at what lay ahead for all of them.

John B. handed another piece of kabana down to Kat, who sat quietly on a reasonably clean portion of carpet under the table. "Jazz, we're gonna just play at being tourists for a bit. You're welcome to join us while you wait."

The engineer considered the offer, which had been endorsed by nods from the others. She smiled. "Thanks guys. I don't want to stray far from town though. It'd be my luck to miss Harlan if he was only back for a flying visit."

When it was next Jazz's turn to go to the bar for a round of drinks, a quiet discussion saw a quick decision by the Canberra group. Wilko took the role of spokesperson when Jazz returned.

"We figure there's enough to see and do round Alice to keep us busy for a few days at least. If you don't mind the company we're happy to stick around and make sure you don't find yourself stranded here."

"Are you sure? I'd appreciate the company. I like meeting locals wherever I travel."

Scarlet shrugged. "We're not exactly locals. Home is a fair way away for all of us, so we're as new to Central Australia as you are."

Wilko and Darren nodded agreement. Nobody noticed John B.'s non-committal silence as he bent to pat Kat.

.o0o.

3 NIGHT SITE

The flames of the small gas stove cast a weird blue light across Drayden's face as he removed the billy. It was a face that wore its characteristic scowl.

"I don't like having to involve him," he growled.

Professor Bevan sighed as he passed his tin mug to his ex-student for filling.

"You know we had, little choice. We needed funds, and a grant from the University was our, only option. It was just unfortunate that they, made it conditional upon, our including our overseas colleague."

"Yeah, why was that? Don't they trust us?"

Bevan tut-tutted. "Dear boy, I doubt that that has, anything to do with it. The submission I prepared should have been, quite satisfactory. No, I suspect that this is a case of, our University grant actually being funded by, American money, perhaps another institution. This will of course have been, contingent upon, the presence of one of their own. The politics and finances of academia are, fraught with such arrangements. I feel I should point out to you that, we have hardly involved Dr. Hunter in our work."

"You seemed keen enough on his opinion when he was here."

"Do I detect a note of, professional jealousy, Mr Drayden? Tut, tut. Hunter is quite well respected as a field archaeologist, particularly in the area of Pacific studies. In the unlikely event that, there were any unpublished reports of discoveries akin to our own, that I didn't know about, he would most assuredly have mentioned them to us when he, saw what we have."

"Yeah, I suppose. I don't like him having seen them, though."

"Calm yourself, dear boy. What could it profit him? He took neither photographs nor record of this site, and even if he had, he rests now in splendid isolation many miles from here. Indeed, many miles from anywhere."

Drayden grinned in response. It wasn't a pleasant grin. "And that's where he'll be staying. When do you reckon we should go back and clean up what's left? There's food and water for a week, maybe two, besides all the empty boxes we left him."

"Oh, perhaps a month. Perhaps a few, weeks more to be on the safe, side."

"Yeah, it's not as if we don't have enough to keep us busy here. You'll contact the Uni then, and advise them of his mysterious disappearance, eh?"

"Mm? Yes." Bevan seemed distracted. Behind his casual reply was the thought, 'when all goes to plan, by that time I will have no need to 'advise' anyone. Of anything.'

"You sure no-one will miss him?"

Drayden's question again interrupted the professor's musings. He replied, "I think not. The academic profile of him that, I checked at the outset indicated, him to be single. Indeed, the paperwork lodged prior, to his joining us here indicated no next, of kin. Contact in case of emergency was, his department head in Hawaii."

"So what we find here remains ours, all ours, eh? Good. What about the European bloke – Krieg?"

"I am confident that Mikkel Krieg will be, as surprised as the rest of the, world by what we achieve here. He did no more than suggest a remote, possibility. The fruits of our, labours shall be as you, say, ours all ours," replied the professor blithely, even if there might have been a trace of insincerity underlying the word 'ours'.

"Bit of luck there," grunted Drayden.

Bevan remained silent. Luck had little to do with it, he believed. It was all down to planning – planning his great destiny.

.o0o.

The little group stood outside the supermarket attempting to devise a mutually acceptable shopping list. Darren and John B. were content with the likes of frozen hamburgers and pizza.

"They're quick and easy," said Darren.

"And while you might not know exactly what it is you're eating, at least you know roughly what it'll taste like," continued Stewart.

"I thought even you took food a little more seriously than that," sniffed Scarlet, who'd been arguing for sensible healthy options.

"Ordinarily, yes," agreed John B., "I'm happy to turn my hand to a chicken Wellington or a chateaubriand, but we're on holiday and I'd rather not work that hard. You better watch your salads, too. We're a long way from home for any lettuce or tomatoes you might find."

 Wilko, ordinarily the fussiest of eaters, was an unlikely mediator.

"Relax guys," he said. "We can suit everyone. John, I'm happy to cook a few meals so we're not paying to eat out all the time. Scarlet, tell me what you will and won't eat and I can knock something together for you, too. I know you're not keen to live on pub food and takeaways."

 Clearly the Tasmanian was getting into Holiday mode. Indeed, he was downright expansive.

"Jazz, what about you? Any special dietary requirements I should know about?"

The blonde engineer returned Wilko's warm smile and said, "I'm happy to take whatever you dish up."

"Okay," replied Wilko, wearing the broadest grin that the others had ever seen on him.

*

Once a mutually acceptable shopping list had been devised Wilko had come up with another suggestion.

"We don't all need to traipse up and down the aisles. Why don't at least some of you head over to the Tourist Information Centre and grab some brochures and stuff on what sort of fun things there are to do around here?"

'Fun things? Is this our Wilko? Either the sun's getting to him, or it's the blonde!' thought John B. to himself.

Jazz piped up, "I'm not sure how much time I'll have to be a real tourist, so I'll give you a hand carrying the food back to the house if you like."

As she made the offer she patted Wilko affectionately on the arm. Stewart could have sworn he saw his Tasmanian friend getting taller.

"We'll do the tourist information thing," said the wizard, with elbow nudges to Scarlet and Darren. "Should we meet back at the house?"

Jazz was looking at a town map mounted on a convenient Information Board.

"Looks like there's a nice park a few blocks over yonder," she said, pointing. "We shouldn't be long, and the house is near here. What's say we pick up some picnic stuff while we're in the supermarket, drop most of the food home, and meet you in the park?"

Scarlet smiled. "That sounds like a lovely idea."

John B. and Darren shrugged.

"Can't see a problem there," agreed the tall youth.

*

And up to a point, there was no problem.

Scarlet, Darren and John B. had a leisurely fossick around the Tourist Information Centre, collecting brochures and investigating a variety of tours lasting from an hour to a 'full day'.

None of the 'full day' tours actually offered twenty-four hours of entertainment, but then, that's the way of advertising. Language is a flexible tool.

The prospect of a 'picturesque Spinifex tour' was quickly dismissed. They'd only just returned from a remote spot in the South Australian desert. There had been moments when they'd feared their last resting place might be under just such a plant. What they wanted now was distraction from unpleasant memories.

Meanwhile, Wilko and Jazz briskly made their way around the supermarket, discovering several culinary common interests as they chatted. Their time flew, even as they unpacked their purchases back at the house.

The point at which a problem revealed itself was when the two groups made their respective ways to the park where they'd planned to picnic. To their chagrin they found the park already populated by a crowd, and it wasn't a happy one.

There was a protest rally under way and it was attracting plenty of attention. It seemed a predominantly local audience, largely but not exclusively Aboriginal.

"The great Scottish poet Robbie Burns once wrote that 'the best-laid plans o' mice and men oft gang aglay', or something like that," stated John B.

"I'm not sure what aglay is, but there seems to be quite a gang here," replied Darren.

"It means 'things go wrong' in English," said Scarlet with some asperity.

"Whatever," Darren shrugged. "I reckon we might have a problem finding Wilko and Jazz in amongst all this lot."

"Well, they might not be head and shoulders above them, but they should stand out in their own way," suggested John B. slightly diplomatically as he eyed the mostly dark-skinned crowd. "Still," he mused, "I wish we could bump into them soon."

Looking for their friends, the three had made their way well past the fringe of the crowd, but weren't particularly focused on the rally itself.

Suddenly a scuffle broke out somewhere nearby and there was an eddy of bodies as people variously tried to get involved or get out of the way. Included among the latter backing hurriedly away from the small melee were a pretty blonde girl and a less-tall-than-he'd-like Tasmanian. They retreated straight into John B. and Darren respectively. Stewart definitely felt he had the better of that circumstance.

"Fancy meeting you here," Stewart grinned.

Scarlet shook her head and sighed. "It's a strange sort of magic you do, but it does seem to work."

Wilko gave her an irritated glance. "Don't encourage him," he said.

Before she could respond it was Scarlet's turn to be collided with, this time by the small but substantial white furry bulk of Kat.

"Time for a strategic retreat?" asked Jazz.

"Reckon so," agreed John B.

"There's some clear space over by that tree," observed Darren, pointing towards a spot that he was tall enough to see over most of the crowd.

The most solidly built of the group, Stewart led the way, bumping like a pinball to leave a wake for the others to follow in. Soon they were sitting or sprawling on the ground under the tree devouring the picnic supplies. Wilko tossed a piece of barbecued chicken to Kat.

The crowd nearby continued to get noisier and rowdier. Wilko stood for a moment to get a glimpse of the speaker who was firing up the mob.

"I reckon that's Carl Costelow," he announced.

"Who?" asked Darren.

"Carl Costelow," Wilko repeated. "I've seen his picture in the papers, here and back in Canberra. Calls himself an aboriginal rights activist – got a reputation as a trouble maker."

"The sort that gives a good cause a bad name," observed Scarlet.

John B. also stood to get a better view.

"He looks about as aboriginal as you do, Scarlet," he said derisively.

The wizard was exaggerating only slightly. While Costelow had a mop of curly hair and some of the facial features common to many aboriginal tribes, the hair was ginger and the skin was touched by only the merest suggestion of dark pigment.

Nonetheless Costelow seemed to be winning the loud support of many of the local indigenous population. As he did, there were some signs of unease among the small contingent of uniformed police and police aides scattered around the edge of the group.

Quietly some of them started to move towards one particular constable, significantly larger than the rest. He had the look of a Viking about him – tall, broad-shouldered and blonde. The handful of other nervous policemen were clearly gathering around him for a small sense of security.

The rabble-rouser bellowed his rhetoric through a megaphone. "It's not enough that we have tourists trampling all over our sacred lands. Now we have archaeologists – white archaeologists – going digging around in our country. Disturbing our past! Our culture! We can't allow them to disturb our precious heritage, our sacred relationship with the land!"

Wilko turned to Jazz and asked, "Is that your boyfriend's lot he's on about, I wonder?"

"I shouldn't think so," Jazz replied. "He's Hawaiian – he's terribly aware of respecting native culture and traditions."

John B. raised an eyebrow. "Yeah, but are the rest of them?"

Costelow continued his harangue.

"He really seems to be trying to stir up a fight, doesn't he?" observed Darren.

"I think he'd find a few willing to oblige," said Wilko, indicating several groups of men making increasingly belligerent noises of support.

Prominent among them, near the stage, was a cluster of hard-looking dark men in denim and leather jackets that bore on the back the words "*Murph's Mob*" and a picture of a skull with one tooth missing. As soon as he opened his mouth to shout agreement with the hectoring Costelow, it was obvious who was the broad-shouldered leader of the Mob – the gap in his gleaming teeth was the match of the artwork on the back of his jacket.

"I reckon I can pick who else will be up for a fight," grumbled John B.

He inclined his head toward the small group of policemen and police aides gathered around the very large blonde constable. He looked more

28

than ever like a Viking who'd swapped his longship and sword for a gym and barbells. He was rolling his shoulders and opening and closing fists like small hams. His belligerent gaze was directed not so much at Costelow as at Murph's milling Mob.

Wilko frowned. "Ordinarily I think you're a bit paranoid about coppers, mate, but I reckon you're right about this one. He looks like trouble waiting to happen."

"And not waiting patiently," said Stewart.

Costelow continued raising the heat of his rhetoric, demanding that, "something must be done about the invaders!"

John B.'s eyes were drawn to the front of the stage. At what seemed a hopefully safe distance from Murph's Mob stood two much older aboriginal men. One was a disheveled figure in clothes several sizes too big for him, stained with sweat, dirt and other things best not considered.

With each sentence Costelow boomed through his megaphone this man looked more and more uncomfortable. His companion though seemed quite unfazed.

He looked to be an even older man. His shirtless wiry frame was clad in worn canvas trousers and an unbuttoned dark waistcoat that carried thick layers of the red dust of the desert. Around his shock of grey frizzled hair was a strip of purple cloth that might once have been a quite natty necktie. His skin, like old sun-baked leather, was several shades darker than most of the dusky brown locals.

"I don't think that motormouth has won over everyone in the crowd," said Stewart.

Darren followed his gaze to look at the two old men and said, "Wow – he's really black, isn't he?"

"Different tribe – different race maybe," the wizard suggested. "There wasn't – isn't – one Aboriginal race you know. A lot of them are as different to each other as they are to Europeans. Look at some of the tribes that used to live down your way in Tasmania, Wilko. There were at least half a dozen completely different types reported, including a tall, very black-skinned bunch who must have looked a lot like that guy."

At that point the man in question turned slightly and met John B.'s gaze, smiled broadly and gave a cheery wave. Stewart gave an uncertain grin and nodded in response.

"That was weird," said Darren looking sideways at the wizard. "Do you know him?"

Stewart shook his head.

"I didn't know you knew so much about aboriginal history," said Wilko, having finally finished chewing and swallowing a thick slab of Turkish bread generously smeared with butter, ham and chilli jam.

Stewart shrugged and said, "Studied it a while ago."

"You're a surprising man sometimes," said Scarlet. "One day I'd like to hear just what you did study before you joined the Public Service."

John B. shrugged again. "A few different things. I got bored easily. When I ran out of stuff I was interested in I moved on to a different course. Ultimately I figured I'd rather be drinking, and that needed a better income than the old student allowance," he admitted.

"Well that bit doesn't surprise me," answered Scarlet sharply.

"Nothing's changed, eh?" said Wilko genially.

John B. looked down to smile at his old friend. Darren nudged his arm. "Here comes that trouble you were worried about," the young man said.

The Nordic-looking policeman had managed to gee up his small band of law-enforcers and was directing them deeper into the crowd. Leading by example, he cleared a path towards the stage by judicious or otherwise application of his truncheon.

With angry shouts Murph's Mob started to make their way toward the police, shoving aside anyone in their way. Murph himself – a youngish man with a broad face and much broader shoulders – produced a set of nunchakus from inside his jacket. He started spinning and flailing them with a proficiency that indicated plenty of practice.

"He's good," remarked Darren, himself a capable if unlikely wielder of weaponry. "Puts on enough of a show to scatter people without actually hitting anyone."

By now the rest of the picnickers had stood up to watch the action, except for Kat who was busy stripping the last shreds of meat from the chicken carcass.

"I don't reckon that's going to be the case much longer," said Jazz in response to Darren's comment.

Murph and the big blonde constable did look to be on a collision course.

"Uh-oh. I think those two old blokes might wind up getting caught in the middle," said Darren with some concern.

As the melee surged and swirled around the two John B. frowned and said, "I wish those two old guys could get safely out of that lot real quick."

Moments later there was a small disturbance at the edge of the crowd near the picnic spot as the two elderly aboriginal men gently but firmly pushed their way out of the crowd.

"T'anks brudder," said the darker man to John B. with a broad grin and a wink.

As he looked at the distance between the stage and where they stood Wilko's mouth worked soundlessly for a moment or two before he was able to ask, "How did you do that?"

The old man chuckled. "You don' get to my age widdout learnin' a few tricks, fella. Hey, you know you look a bit like one a dem goldfishes when you do dat?"

"So I've heard," Wilko replied, nodding.

"Are you gentlemen alright?" asked Scarlet.

"Yeah. Yeah, right," mumbled the lighter skinned man, who seemed almost as bemused as Wilko.

"I think it's time we packed up and scarpered," suggested Jazz.

"Good idea," agreed John B. Turning to their new acquaintances he asked, "Can we buy you blokes a drink?"

"Yeah, reckon so," said the disheveled man, brightening at the prospect.

His darker companion nudged him with his elbow, though, and said, "Possum – I thought you reckoned you'd made a promise to yourself you weren't ever gonna drink wid someone you don' know again."

The man addressed as Possum looked unhappily back at the stage and replied, "Well, yeah… but I reckon these here folks are alright."

"Thanks," said John B.

"An' I reckon you're right. Dey good people. But a promise is a promise, an' if you can't keep one you make to yourself, how's anyone else ever gonna trust you?" The old man turned to the group and said, "T'anks again folks. We gonna be gettin' on." He looked at each of the group in turn with twinkling appraising eyes.

Patting John B. on the arm he said, "Smart cat you got dere. Be seeing you."

With that, the old man led Possum away through the trees and out of the park.

"What an interesting chap," said Scarlet.

"No bad vibes about him?" John B. asked her a little playfully, remembering some of her inquisitorial reactions to his early claims of magical powers.

"Not at all," replied Scarlet with great seriousness.

"Yeah. Nice old codger," agreed Jazz.

"Goldfish. Harrumph. And bloody 'magic' again," grumbled Wilko, but it was a good-natured grumble.

They gathered up their bits and pieces. Stewart picked up Kat who purred loudly then promptly fell asleep in his arms. With cautious haste they left the park and the rally, not giving a backward glance to the impending confrontation between Murph and the big blonde constable.

The little band of travelers made their way back to the house for an afternoon and evening of board games, television, picnic leftovers, quiet drinks from a handy bottle shop, and a lot of amiable conversation.

.oOo.

5 GETTING THE HUMP

The next day dawned bright and clear, as they usually do in Central Australia. The aroma of breakfast being cooked by Wilko quickly lured the others from their rooms, although nobody was at the table before Kat.

Wilko shook his head. "He's impressive. I walked in here, took the bacon out of the fridge, turned around and there he was – sitting up on the chair, one paw on the table."

"He's got an instinct for food," said John B. with a shrug. "When he started yowling with that note he gets in his voice when he senses tucker, I figured it was time to get up - I knew you'd be cooking soon."

It was a hearty meal of varying proportions of fried bacon and eggy bread. A small portion, with lashings of side salad, satisfied Scarlet. Jazz surprised everyone by splashing nearly as much hot chilli sauce on her breakfast as Wilko. A legacy of working in Africa, she explained.

"Remind me please, someone, what time do we set out on today's adventure?" asked John B. after they'd eaten.

Scarlet consulted the booking sheet they'd been given at the Tourist Information Centre the previous day.

She replied, "We're to be at the Information Centre at 10.30 to meet the minibus that will take us out to the camel farm. After an enjoyable visit there we will have a leisurely and unique camel trek out to the Old

Telegraph Station and back."

Jazz smiled. "Those bloody travel brochure things sound the same all the world, don't they?"

"Might not be the best day out for you, mate," said John B. to Kat as he scratched the back of the feline form draped across his lap.

The white Persian looked up and gave a half-purring "Mreh." He slipped off Stewart's lap and went to stretch out on a cool patch of lino beside his plate. He clearly expected this to be filled enough to amuse him in everyone's absence.

"Right, that's settled," said Stewart. "I suppose we better get ready."

"Hats and sunscreen all round," warned Scarlet.

There was agreement from everyone – none of them had complexions that were ideally suited to the Central Australian desert. Indeed, to judge by the weathered appearance of the two old men they'd met the day before, it seemed there really wasn't an 'ideal' complexion. Any human skin was ultimately vulnerable to the baking heat and ultra-violet rays.

Jazz, Scarlet and Darren donned broad-brimmed straw hats, while John B. and Wilko put on rabbit-skin felt Akubra bush hats. Equipped with water bottles all round they set out to enjoy the day.

*

A little while later, they had learned more about camels than they had thought possible, or indeed perhaps desirable. For instance, they were told that a beast weighing over 800 pounds could drink a hundred litres of water in less than two minutes.

Wilko looked thoughtful. "If my mental arithmetic is still any good, I reckon that's about the same rate that I've seen you knock off a good shot of single malt Scotch, John."

"I don't think it sustains him as long as the water does for the camel," observed Scarlet.

Jazz chuckled, not least at Stewart's look of injured innocence as the wizard replied, "Since when did you two start comparing notes?"

Soon after, the five companions were part of a fifteen-strong 'camel train' that ambled its way across the sands outside Alice Springs.

Their "tour leader" was a pretty young man with more ego than intelligence, and a penchant for attractive blonde women. Having completely failed to win the interest of Jazz, he'd turned his attentions to a young German tourist. The fraulein spoke little English and found the Australian accent almost impenetrable, but since the young man was far more interested in the sound of his own voice the one-sided nature of the 'conversation' didn't bother him.

After "traditional billy tea and damper with Golden syrup" – that mainstay of the outback tourism industry – at the old Telegraph Station, the 'camel train' set out for the four or five kilometre trip back to the camel farm.

It was mid-afternoon, and the sun was as unrelenting as expected. The saving grace of the weather was a steady breeze that cooled the sweaty skin of the fourteen camel riders and their guide.

The convoy gradually strung out along the track, some in little conversational clusters. Others were riding alone, either to enjoy the solitude and the view, or because their camel wasn't feeling sociable.

The tour leader was at the front, deeply engrossed in trying to impress the bemused fraulein. Jazz and Scarlet were riding side by side, discussing history, from the local area to some of the lore of magic. Nearby Darren and John B. had gotten into idle conversation with a couple of other holiday-makers.

Some way behind the 'train' rode Wilko. His camel, a surly creature with the unlikely name of Buttercup, had steadily slowed down until she moved at barely more than a plod. The others had progressively overtaken them and now man and beast were lagging well to the rear.

"I think you're running out of gas, Buttercup," the Tasmanian suggested. He tapped the animal's hump. "Feels full," he said with a chuckle to himself.

Buttercup turned her head back to look at her passenger, snorted as if in reply to Wilko's little witticism, and came to a complete stop.

"Hey, come on girl – giddy up… or something! Don't just stand here!"

The camel stood, impassive and unmoving. Wilko tried rapping her sides with his heels, slapping her on the rump, even shouting at her, all to no avail. The riders ahead were rounding a mound of rocks and one by one were being lost to view.

"So Jazz, what did you think of the Telegraph Station?" asked Scarlet.

"Interesting in its way, I guess. The wallabies were nice. I still find it funny though when Aussies talk about 'early history' in buildings built in the 1870s. I mean, my local pub back home is three hundred years older than that!"

"Really?" exclaimed Scarlet in surprise.

"Yeah – the White Swan. Nice old place – I'll have to take you there for a drink one day."

"Um – well…"

"Not to worry Scarlet, I'll have yours for you," grinned John B. "And I'm sure Wilko could be talked into it!"

Darren looked around and asked, "Where is Wilko, anyway?"

Stewart looked back and shrugged. "Behind and getting behinder. I think Buttercup may be running out of gas."

Jazz laughed and replied, "I've never known a shortage of gas to be a problem for a camel!"

"Fair call," agreed the wizard. Right on cue the camel he was riding – 'Orange' by name if not quite by coloration – let rip a loud fart.

"Well, yours certainly seems to be full of it!" observed Darren.

Jazz giggled and said "That's a good description of our bloody guide, if you ask me!"

"Certainly some of his comments about the aboriginal children schooled at the station from the 1930s were less than polite," said Scarlet.

"That's putting it mildly," agreed Jazz.

"You know, that's been niggling at me ever since he made his first off-colour remark…"

"Scarlet! Was that a pun?"

"No John, it certainly wasn't! Well, not deliberately. I might feel better if I go and have some words with that young man," said Scarlet with a feisty look on her face. So saying, she flicked the reins of her camel, who obligingly broke into a trot in the direction of the tour guide.

Darren grinned. "I reckon this might be worth watching," he said, encouraging his camel to follow her.

Sadly, Darren was doomed to disappointment as Scarlet proved unable to engage the guide in conversation. The young man was too much impressed with himself – his appearance and what he regarded as his wit – to recognize the extent to which he was boring the young German backpacker who, he considered, was nearly as pretty as he was. Certainly, he thought, she was attractive enough to be more worthy of his attentions than the bespectacled woman who wanted to berate him like an angry hen, clearly not 'getting' his humour.

Meanwhile, Jazz took the opportunity to ask John B. about how his 'magic' worked.

"Honestly, I don't really know. It just does. I wish for stuff, and somehow it happens. The emphasis is on somehow – I don't reckon I can control how the 'stuff' actually happens. Jeez – I can't even predict it," admitted the wizard.

"Sounds – I don't know – not very helpful?" said the blonde.

"Oh, it's helpful enough. Just unpredictable." At that moment, a gust of wind caught Stewart's broad-brimmed hat and sent it spinning back along the sandy track.

"I wish I didn't lose my hat," was John B.'s immediate response.

One of the trailing camels obligingly stepped on the hat, squashing it into the soft sand but certainly stopping its progress.

"Well, it's a bit barmy but your magic does seem to work.," said Jazz.

"Yeah, whatever Wilko may say. But that's the problem y'see. I don't control how it works."

John B. directed Orange back along the track to where his hat was half buried. The camel knelt. With a little sigh he brushed the sand off the hat and pushed it back into something as close to its original shape as he could manage.

"Thanks, mate," said the wizard, patting the obliging camel on the shoulder. It chewed impassively.

Stewart jammed the hat back down on his head. Orange stood back up and, at a canter, brought her rider back alongside Jazz and her mount.

The engineer was shaking her head in bemusement as he rode up. "Oh, by the way John, did you see Wilko back there?" she asked.

"No," was the reply. "He must be a fair way back. I hope he's alright."

*

Wilko drummed his fingers on Buttercup's neck. "Amazing," he said to the camel. "We've just been told the wild camels of Australia have such a pure bloodline, are so healthy, and are so all-round bloody excellent that we're exporting your kin to the Arabs for squillions of dollars. And here you are, standing around like a bottle of rum at an AA meeting." His voice rose to a shout, "Will you bloody well move!?!"

The camel turned her head to look back at her passenger. She looked him in the eye, farted thunderously, and then took off at a trot. Unfortunately for Wilko the trot was in the wrong direction.

As he bounced helplessly in the saddle, bright red with frustration, the Tasmanian took off his hat and flailed it at the back of Buttercup's neck. As they cleared the crest of a sand dune and started heading down the other side at speed he leaned forward and bellowed into the camel's ear, "You know, I've read that if you marinate camel haunch for a while it makes a bloody good stew."

Buttercup's big feet dug into the sand and she came to a sudden stop. Already leaning forward, Wilko pitched over her head and performed a creditable barrel roll into what luckily was a soft sand drift.

He lay spread-eagled on his back looking up at Buttercup. The camel returned his gaze, blinking slowly.

"Right," said Wilko. "So we have a bit of an understanding now, do we? Okay – what now? I don't suppose you're going to be co-operative enough to explain to me how I'm supposed to climb back on board?"

Buttercup blinked again.

"Great," muttered Wilko. "It was bad enough when I started talking to Kat. Now here I am trying to converse with a camel!"

'Okay', Wilko thought to himself. 'I know which direction they went in. If I can spot them I might just be able to get their attention.' He identified the tallest of the nearby sand hills and clambered up. A single rider was visible.

Wilko stood on top of the dune shouting at the rider of the last camel in the train.

"Oi!! Oi!! I'm stuck back here! Wait for me! Come back! Hey!" he shouted to no avail.

The teenage girl on the last camel was nearly as far behind the rest of the train as Wilko and Buttercup had been behind her. She was utterly bored by the day's outing, which had been foisted on her by parents keen to have a day to themselves while ensuring she spent some time in healthy fresh air.

To amuse herself she had brought her mp3 player on the trip. With Scream Club playing at high volume in her earphones she was entirely oblivious to the camels some distance in front of her and the shouts of the Tasmanian even further behind.

As the girl and her camel disappeared from his view around a bend in the track Wilko groaned, "You stupid bimbo..."

Buttercup the camel ambled up the dune and with apparent care plodded past Wilko to provide a patch of shade for him to stand in. Her erstwhile rider looked up at her and said ruefully, "Well, thanks for that, at least."

While the camel stood chewing placidly, Wilko stood with hands on hips looking unhappily into the distance. After a couple of minutes his brow creased as he tried to identify an odd noise. It was a rhythmic whiff whiff whiff with small squeaking sounds underlying it.

The source suddenly appeared. Through a gap in a nearby ridge of sand came a jogger – a thin figure soaked in sweat, dressed in brief running shorts and a singlet, with wraparound sunglasses and a t-shirt tied round the top of his head as some sort of sun protection.

'Either the heat's fried my brain and I'm hallucinating, or there's someone out here who's actually crazier than I am' thought Wilko. 'Hang on… I know that face! It can't be, surely?' Uncertainly he called out, "Rod! Rod! Up here!"

Wilko scratched his head and said, "Y'know Buttercup, I'd swear that was a bloke I used to work with years ago. He was a runner, I remember – Roderick Drayden his name was."

The camel spat a glob of vile-smelling liquid into the sand.

"Hey! Hey! Mate! Stop, will ya?!" shouted Wilko as he slipped and slid, trying to run down the dune to intercept the jogger. The Tasmanian's feet went out from under him and he rolled in a cloud of red sand. He looked up through the swirling particles to see the runner continuing on, apparently oblivious to him.

Long distance runners talk about 'the zone' – a point where their concentration is so focused on their running that they lose all awareness of anything else around them. Wilko had heard of this phenomenon, and bitterly concluded that this was why he'd failed to get a reaction. He peered at the departing figure, striding between dunes away to the west of the track taken by the camel train.

As he struggled to his feet and started to brush sand off himself he mused, 'I'm sure I recognize that face.' Looking up he realized that Buttercup had strolled down the dune and was once more providing welcome shade for him.

"Thanks again," he said courteously. "I just hope I'm not stuck out here too long. No offence, but there's another girl with long eyelashes I'd rather be talking to."

Buttercup grunted.

Wilko would have been comforted to know that, some distance ahead, his absence had been well and truly noticed by the girl he was talking about.

Jazz had to shout to get the attention of the guide who was still engrossed in trying to endear himself to the attractive fraulein from Frankfurt.

"Hey, fearless leader! We're a man down!" called the English girl.

"What are you talking about?" came the irritated reply.

"We're missing one of the group," Jazz answered through gritted teeth.

The guide waved an irritated hand. "That's impossible. I've never lost anyone on one of my tours."

"Do a head count then, you dill," shouted John B. "Where's Wilko?"

"Red and white striped beanie and t-shirt? Big glasses? Oh no, that's Where's Wally, isn't it?" said the guide, smiling winningly at the German girl who looked at him blankly.

"No," said Scarlet. "Pale blue t-shirt, light brown hat and sunglasses."

The guide frowned. "It was just my little joke…" He saw the look on Scarlet's face. "Never mind."

Hearing the exchange, the rest of the group were reining in their camels and starting to gather around the guide.

Quickly counting heads, John B. confirmed, "Fourteen including you. We're a man short."

"A short man short!" chortled the guide, once again trying to demonstrate his wit.

"I don't think that's appropriate, do you?" asked Scarlet coldly, once again causing the pretty young man to squirm uncomfortably in his saddle.

Jazz turned to the bored teenager who had been riding ahead of Wilko and had just caught up with the group. The engineer said, "You were riding at the back – did you see or hear anything?"

The girl looked blank, still unable to hear anything but Scream Club and not even vaguely aware someone was talking to her. Jazz gee-ed her camel over to the girl, reached across and plucked off the headphones. *Distracted* was all too clearly audible.

"Did you see what happened to Wilko?" demanded Jazz.

"Hey! Who? Giz me earphones back!" cried the girl indignantly.

"Bloody air thief," snarled the blonde engineer and tossed the earphones back.

Darren was looking back along the track. "We better go back and find him," he said.

"He's probably still at the Telegraph Station scoffing leftovers. I don't think he was ever with us. I think you counted wrong," spluttered the guide in growing agitation.

John B. was also looking back the way they'd come. "I think you're right, Darren. Should only take a couple of us though – the rest go on and we'll catch up."

The guide trotted his camel over then reached to seize Stewart's arm. "No separating the group! We'll consider this when we get back to the farm!" he declared pompously.

The wizard looked at the plaster cast on his hand, then up at the guide's perfect teeth. Very calmly he said, "I am going to ride back and find my mate. I wish I didn't have to thump you to make that happen."

With commendable accuracy Jazz's camel spat a stream of well-chewed foul black goop into the face of the guide. The entire group (most noticeably the German girl) laughed uproariously as he shrieked and wiped frantically at his face. The vile stuff was running down his previously pristine Authentic Western-Style shirt.

"Aaagh! Aaagh! Do what you like!" the young man babbled, turning his mount and taking off in the direction of the camel farm, where he would shortly be receiving instruction to seek employment elsewhere. It was an instruction he would accept willingly, the taste and smell of camel spit still lingering in his mouth and up his nose.

"I'll ride with you, John," said Jazz.

"The four of us will stick together," announced Scarlet, unexpectedly taking charge. "The rest of you better follow… that man."

Darren grinned and remarked, "It looks like a lot of the flies have already decided to. That's no bad thing."

So the nine other tourists dutifully trotted off on the trail of the man already being popularly called Stinkface. The wizard and his companions urged their camels back the way they'd come.

After several minutes riding they heard a loud grateful "Helloooo!"

Some distance away they saw Wilko, now sitting atop a dune in the shade of the obliging Buttercup, waving his hat at them.

They soon covered the distance and stopped beside the Tasmanian.

"I'm bloody glad to see you!" exclaimed Jazz. The others all expressed similar sentiments, but nothing would top the broad smile that creased Wilko's face when the English girl had spoken first.

John B. said something to Buttercup and she dutifully knelt to allow her erstwhile rider to climb back on board.

Wilko shook his head. "I know we got told that command back at the farm, but I'm blowed if I can remember it."

"Yeah, we did, didn't we?" said Stewart vaguely as he patted Buttercup's nose.

"You know, I never doubted you guys would turn up, but where's the tour guide? And the rest of the tour, for that matter?" asked Wilko.

"They're headed back to the camel farm," replied Scarlet.

"That bloody creep…" Jazz began to mutter.

"I think he got what he deserved," Scarlet interrupted.

Jazz grinned at the memory and replied "Not half!"

Wilko looked puzzled.

"Funny story," said Darren. "We'll tell you on the way home."

"Speaking of funny," replied Wilko, "I saw the damnedest thing while I was waiting here. I'm sure it wasn't a mirage – they're meant to be attractive…"

The little group headed back to the farm, swapping stories of camel spit and an unlikely jogger.

50

.oOo.

6 PERSISTENCE OF SITE

Not for the first time Harlan looked back over his shoulder, almost longingly, at the jumble of large stones behind him.

He stretched his legs and rolled his shoulders, thinking wistfully for a moment that a back massage would be nice. That triggered a guilty thought – he'd meant to send a message for Jazz to the Post Office via one of the other two archaeologists. Ah well, he'd sort that out next time he saw them. Or perhaps he'd get a lift back into town with them.

Careless though – he should have left a message before he set off. He'd intended to do so, but the significance of Professor Bevan's find had just seemed so great that he'd been preoccupied. And as it turned out it looked as though he was right.

A few of the large stones stood up like the fingers of a hand. These were at the edge of an expanse of flat stones that sloped away under the sands. There were carvings at the base of the standing stones, and more visible on the sloping surface. It was clear that Harlan had begun sweeping away sand to uncover more of them.

These were rather better preserved than the eroded few that Bevan had first pointed out to him.

But with a gesture of determination he turned away from the carvings and sat back down to look at the sketch pad on his lap.

"Focus. Focus. One job at a time. Those aren't going anywhere. Focus!" he said to himself.

 Closing his eyes he once again called to mind the carvings he'd seen at Bevan's 'primary' site. With a small satisfied nod he opened his eyes and drew another symbol on the pad. A photographic memory was a handy thing sometimes.

.oOo.

Repeated checks at the Post Office over a couple of days still brought no news of Harlan. It had reached the point where Jazz didn't even need to queue. If one of the counter staff saw her come through the doorway they would just shake their head or shrug apologetically.

It was causing increasing annoyance to Jazz, and a small measure of unspoken pleasure for Wilko, sympathetic as he truly was to her concern. This was because the continued absence of her boyfriend meant she was spending her time with their little group, and seemed to be particularly enjoying the company of the Tasmanian. The feeling was mutual.

The group, including Kat this time, had spent a chunk of this latest day at Pitchi Richi enjoying a pioneer museum, sculptures and a native flower garden. Wilko had dropped everyone at the pub, parked his Triumph at the house, and was walking the short distance to rejoin his friends over a drink.

He strolled up the street, whistling an old blues tune to himself, although any blues fan would have struggled to recognize it. Suddenly out of the doorway of a pharmacy in front of him stepped the jogger he'd spotted from the sand dune.

"Roderick! Rod Drayden! It bloody well is you! I thought I recognized you the other day," exclaimed Wilko.

The lean figure looked up in shock. He stared at the shorter man for a moment, and then recognition dawned.

"Wilkes. Robert Wilkes, isn't it?" he said. "You were in Canberra, when I was still stuck behind a desk."

"That's right! You did get out completely, then? I remember you going off to study… something," prompted Wilko.

"Too bloody right! No going back there!"

If Wilko noticed that Drayden's voice was more aggressive than good natured he chose to ignore it, saying, "I'm in town on holidays with some mates – why don't you join us for a drink and you can tell me what brings you out to the Alice?"

A dismissive reply died on Drayden's lips as he contemplated the delightful prospect of another evening across the campfire from Walter Bevan. A few beers suddenly seemed attractive – a long-denied guilty pleasure.

"Yeah. Alright – why not?" said the archaeologist.

They entered the pub and walked up to the bar together. Wilko looked over to his friends' table, checking that everyone appeared to have a drink in front of them. Satisfied, he asked Drayden, "What'll you have, Rod?"

"Roderick. A schooner."

Wilko shrugged, ignoring the absence of courtesy. "Whatever. Sure – coming up," he said. "Two schooners and a packet of chips, please," he said to the barmaid.

"Salt and vinegar," Drayden said.

The barmaid raised a questioning eyebrow to Wilko who shrugged and nodded. Once served, Wilko paid up then led the way to the table where his companions waited. Drayden sat in the vacant chair while Wilko pulled up another for himself.

"Cheers everyone," said Wilko. "This is an old workmate of mine: Rod – Roderick Drayden. John, you might remember him. Charlotte, a bit before your time, I think." Going around the table, he introduced Jazz and Darren.

John B. nodded. "Yeah. You left soon after I came down from Brisbane."

Wilko smiled at a memory. "I remember we used to call you 'Drano' didn't we?"

"From Drayden – yeah, that makes sense," said Darren.

"Coincidence," averred John B. "Actually he was called Drano because he was clean round the bend."

There were chuckles all round the table. Well, all except from the chair Drayden occupied.

"Yeah, I do remember you," said Roderick, sneering at Stewart. "The hippy no-hoper."

"Indeed," nodded John B., sounding almost acquiescent. "I should have had higher hopes. I should, for example, have hoped I wouldn't see you again.”

Unfortunately the conversation continued in a similar vein. Wilko found himself feeling trapped. On the one hand, having invited Roderick to join them he felt some obligation to defend his ex-colleague – or at least not join in the verbal sniping. On the other hand, Drayden was being so determinedly unpleasant he couldn't blame the others for getting irritated. Any attempts they'd made to lighten the atmosphere between Stewart and Drayden had been scuppered on the rocks of the latter's sharp tongue.

Darren had simply asked, “Wow – were the two of you like this when you had to work together?”

“Work? This slob?” responded Drayden. “And you keep out of this, Junior. Talking to you would be a battle of wits with an unarmed opponent.”

John B. snorted contemptuously. “ That's rich coming from a bloke so stupid mind-readers only charge half price.”

“ Really?” said Darren. “That's nice of them given how small the print must be.”

“They'd be giving you a refund!” retorted Drayden.

Scarlet decided to try to defuse matters. “Oh stop it you lot. You sound like a bunch of schoolboys.”

Drayden looked her up and down, then responded with a sneer, “I don't reckon you'd remember what a schoolboy sounded like.”

As Wilko squirmed uncomfortably, Jazz returned from buying her round at the bar. She'd been standing behind Drayden and Wilko holding a loaded tray listening to the exchange.

The blonde engineer proffered drinks to Wilko, Scarlet, John B. and Darren, then carefully put her own glass on the table. With considerably less grace she thumped Drayden's schooner in front of him, slopping beer onto the table.

With a sweet smile she said, "Oops – sorry mate. Now then, you obviously didn't get into stand-up comedy. What did you leave your desk job to do?"

"I went to University. Got a Masters, majoring in archaeology," was the smug reply.

Wilko raised a surprised eyebrow and said, "That's a surprising choice."

Drayden shrugged. "I was very good at History in school. Excellent in fact. There's money in antiquities. And it's outdoor work. Better than getting fat and lazy in an office."

Jazz smiled. An alert man, who Roderick Drayden wasn't, would have noticed that it was a very superficial smile.

The pretty blonde nodded and replied to him, "I understand about the outdoor work – it's why I do the job I do. So, archaeology brings you to this part of the world? I wouldn't have thought there were a lot of valuable antiquities around here."

"You'd be surprised!" snorted the archaeologist.

"Ah, dere's lots o' surprises round dis place!"

Everyone around the table jumped in surprise (only the heights varied) – nobody had noticed the old aboriginal man arrive to stand beside their table. He gave an amiable grin.

John B. raised a glass in greeting, but it was Darren who spoke first. "Hey – you're the old black guy we met in the park, at that rally. Sorry, that was rude – I don't remember your name…"

The old man's grin widened. "Old Black Guy sounds about right I reckon," he said.

"You want to pull up a chair and join us?" invited John B. "I know you don't drink – alcohol anyway, but neither does Scarlet. You're still welcome."

"T'anks brudder. Y'know, I never said I don' drink. Jus' reminded ol' Possum of a promise he made to himself. Me, I'll have a good whisky I reckon. Don' you worry, I'll get it myself," said Guy, still smiling.

He went to the bar, walking in a long easy stride that told of many years of loping across the desert. The barman gave the old man a respectful nod along with a generous measure of good single malt. No money changed hands.

Drayden sneered in the direction of the bar and said, "Of course, not everything that's ancient is valuable."

Scarlet gave him what she hoped was a penetrating stare. "Valuable antiquities? Is that what that loud fellow in the park was talking about? You're one of the group supposedly working on sacred land north of here."

"Bloody prof and I are the only ones doing any bloody work around here," muttered Drayden curtly and mostly to himself.

"Really?" asked Jazz innocently. "Well, if you're the only working archaeologists around here you must know my boyfriend. Harlan Hunter."

Drayden took his time draining his glass before replying, "Never heard of him."

"Oh come on," replied Jazz, much more mildly than she felt. "Medium height, dark hair and beard – well, perhaps a bit of silver in it. American accent. How big is your team?"

"It's not. Just me and old man Bevan. I told you. Never heard of Harley Hunt." For a moment the archaeologist tried to meet the fixed gaze of Jazz but found he couldn't.

Stewart was holding his whisky glass on its side. He observed idly, "You ever noticed that you can't do that with a full one?"

"What's that supposed to mean?" snapped Drayden, less grateful than he should have been for the distraction.

"Your round, Longpockets," Stewart replied.

Scarlet frowned and repeated, "Longpockets?"

"Long pockets. Short arms. Can't seem to reach his wallet," explained John B.

Drayden looked around the table quickly, an ugly scowl on his face. "You're joking," he said. "Wilkes dragged me in here for a drink. You don't think I'd pay to be in the company of any of you lot, do you? I got shopping to do."

With that the surly archaeologist stood and left the tavern, not quite at his running pace but walking at a speed that indicated a great enthusiasm to be elsewhere.

With a growl Stewart made to get up from his chair. Old Black Guy, standing behind him, put a hand on his shoulder.

Darren also put a hand on the wizard's arm and said, "He's not worth going to the watch-house for."

"Yeah. Yeah, you're right," agreed John B. "They're not a fun place to spend any time."

Wilko looked at his old friend sideways and said, "I'll take your word for it. Listen everyone, sorry for inflicting him on you – I don't remember him being quite so aggro. He's right though, I brought him in here. I'll get his round."

"Like hell you will!" said Jazz sharply. "We'll all get our own. Don't worry about a tray, I'll help you carry them."

Everyone around the table duly handed over their contribution for the next round of drinks.

To Wilko's unspoken delight Jazz took his arm as they went to the bar and said quietly in his ear, "Don't you let a bugger like that get you down. You were trying to be a mate – not your fault he turned out how he bloody did. You deserved better just for making the effort."

Back at the table Scarlet observed, "I'm very glad I never had to put up with the sound of his voice in the office!"

"I wish one day he'd shut up for good!" growled John B.

With uncharacteristic bitterness Darren agreed. "You should have been more specific. Like, today."

The wizard sighed and nodded. "Probably. Ah well – his time will come."

"Yeah, reckon you right," agreed Old Black Guy as he patted Stewart on the arm.

*

Back outside the Tavern Drayden was stalking towards the supermarket. He almost collided with Carl Costelow who'd been briskly striding in the opposite direction.

For a moment both men stood still, each waiting for the other to apologise for getting in the way. That wasn't going to happen.

The activist lawyer looked hard at the lean man facing him. Where had he seen him before? Yes – loitering outside his office when the old man from the University had first arrived asking unusual questions.

"You work with that archaeologist Bevan, don't you? His assistant or something?"

"I'm a bloody archaeologist myself mate! And a bloody good one! By the time I get done at Cobbemarmoo everyone's gonna bloody know it, too. What we're sittin' on up there…"

Drayden's voice tailed off. He had no idea who he was talking to, but suddenly realised he was talking too much. Didn't matter. Bloody professor would never know, would he?

"Sounds interesting," began Costelow, but before he could learn more the chance encounter was over. The archaeologist just grunted, pushed his way past and continued up the street.

The lawyer stood for a moment and watched him go.

"Sounds quite interesting," he said quietly.

.o0o.

8 TROUBLED SITE

The sky was still light, although it wouldn't be for much longer, when Drayden parked the four-wheel-drive at the Cobbemarmoo campsite he shared with Bevan.

It was clear that the excavation was progressing at some pace. The increasing size of the mounds of relocated sand was testimony to that.

So too was the fact that it was no longer necessary to bend double to move around some of the space under the rock shelf where the carvings were found.

Drayden had hoped he'd hit the cave floor the first time his shovel clanked on a hard stone surface. That proved not to be the case though, and he was irritated to find many of his subsequent barrowfuls of sand further weighed down by fragments of broken flat sandstone slab.

Some were fist sized, others about the diameter of a dinner plate, and one was a large irregularly shaped piece the size of a doormat.

The professor wasn't visible as his protégé climbed out of the cabin. 'Old coot's probably in his cave,' thought Drayden as he slammed the truck's door.

At the sound of the slam Bevan emerged from the cave just as Drayden was removing shopping bags from the back of the vehicle. The older man was clutching a small brush and a notebook.

"You're later than I, anticipated," observed the professor with surprisingly little trace of irritation.

"Got side-tracked in town. Met up with someone I haven't seen in a long time."

"Really? Another of my ex-students perchance?"

"No, further back, when I was still a public servant," Drayden replied without looking up from unpacking tins of food.

"Ah – before you found your, true calling."

"Whatever you reckon."

The professor was in an unusually amiable mood. The inscriptions he'd clearly been studying in the cave had obviously lifted his spirits. Drayden didn't think twice about dispelling the good humour.

He said, "We've got a problem. Hunter's been missed."

Bevan looked at him in puzzlement. The younger man explained.

"He's got a bunch of mates in town. I just happened to bump into them. I used to work with a couple of them – they recognised me."

"From the public, service? Here in Australia? Strange. How do they, come to know Dr. Hunter?"

"Dunno. One of the birds reckoned she was his girlfriend. English, by the sound of her."

Bevan's relative cheeriness had been successfully dashed.

"Blast!" he snapped, which was as close to swearing as he normally came. "What did you tell her – them?"

Drayden shrugged and replied, "Nothing. Said I'd never heard of him."

"Hmm…" The professor fixed a piercing gaze on his assistant and asked, "How much do, they know about what, we're doing here?"

Another shrug. "Nothing as far as I know. I didn't tell them anything. They know there's something going on because they know the Yank's supposed to be out here. And because they heard some bloke at a rally in town running his mouth about digging on a sacred site."

Bevan slammed the brush down hard on a table top as he snapped, "That fool Costelow. When the University insisted I, check on the actual, ownership of this, land, consulting a local lawyer seemed the easiest way of, doing so. I didn't think I'd, said anything to arouse his aggravation or, even interest though."

He folded his arms, inhaled and exhaled heavily for a few moments. Drayden watched with something like wry amusement until the older man snapped at him, "Hurry up with those provisions. Light the gas lamps. When that's done you can, take over from me in, the cave. Open up more of that back corner while I, prepare dinner."

"I'm not hungry," Drayden said, sounding like a petulant child.

"Then don't eat. Get by on the beer I smell on, your breath. I notice you've also acquired yourself a, bottle of rum – raising your, spirits perhaps?"

"You got a problem with that?"

"No, though not overly fond of distilled burnt sugar myself I've spent my share of, time enjoying good ale in public houses. Indeed we would not be, here if not for the, information I picked up in such, an establishment."

Drayden smiled his mirthless grin. "Right enough. That reminds me, Hunter's mates had an old black codger with them, too. Not the bloke you were talking to that time. An even older one I reckon."

"Hmm. I wonder what knowledge he, might have imparted?" the professor mused.

"Nothing worthwhile if I'm any judge," was the surly reply.

"Really? Mm. To work, Mr. Drayden. I will consider, the problem for now. Meanwhile, you might consider how centaurs ruined an Italian civilization."

Bevan picked his brush back up, carefully blew sand particles from its bristles, and strode back to the cave. Drayden picked up a tin of beans and shaped to throw it at the back of the professor's head.

Instead he snorted his annoyance and said to himself, "Bloody centaurs?! I hate it when he does that!"

Bevan's voice came from under the sandstone ledge. "Etruscan, Mr. Drayden. A simple anagram."

The professor neither heard nor saw the snarl that was his only reply. Away from his assistant's view he allowed himself to give vent to his own aggravation.

He muttered to himself, "There are moments when, I almost wish I'd stayed a primary school teacher. Those little ratbags, were easier to keep, in their place. Even the smartest of them could be put, down with a question that you knew, was too hard for them. Nothing like seeing a little smart-alec realize they didn't, know everything. Kids, today, think they're so smart."

He continued to brush sand from faint inscriptions on the cavern floor and wall. His mind wandered back to the time when, as a relatively young man, he committed himself to enough years of determined study to go from school teaching to lecturing.

It had allowed him to specialize – concentrate his efforts firstly on his favourite subject, ancient history, and then on his specific interest. Others might have defined that as the rise and fall of civilizations. Bevan was more precisely interested in the gain and loss of power. Why had certain cultures or certain leaders attained prominence, and what had prevented them from holding it indefinitely?

He should have been a pure researcher, happiest in his own company and that of copious quantities of obscure source materials. Unfortunately that didn't pay the bills.

Walter Bevan wasn't a man of expensive tastes, but he'd come to academia from what would be called an underprivileged background. The family farm had, over generations, run too many sheep on too little land. The pasture steadily disappeared. Without it, more of the topsoil blew away with every decent wind. The sheep gradually died off, and neither old Wilfred nor Walter's father Winston Bevan had the flexibility of outlook to consider any alternative produce until the ground was simply too poor to support anything.

Winston's one hope for the future was his son. His wife had inconveniently died soon after the boy was born, so there'd be no others to pin his hopes on. Winston knew he had nothing to offer a potential new bride, even one of those foreign ones he'd heard neighbours boast of buying from newspaper ads. 'Nothin' to buy 'er with,' he'd mused after listening to old Peterson from over the hill gloat about the Eastern European beauty who'd be arriving for him soon. ('Beauty' turned out to be very much in the eye of the beholder. Luckily old Peterson had truly terrible eyesight.)

The aging farmer Bevan instead devoted what little money he had – mostly government support – to the furthering of young Walter's studies. He couldn't afford expensive boarding schools, but as best he could he bankrolled the boy's prodigious appetite for reading.

By the time Winston died his son had just finished school. Teacher's College was a much more affordable option than the University that Walter craved. Winston's passing, and the inheritance of the farm, brought only debts that just added to the young man's parlous financial position.

It only fuelled his determination. He would make his way in the world using his brains, as his father had demanded. He would find a way to be powerful, instead of powerless. He lived frugally while the meagre government student support saw him through College.

A primary school teacher's salary was one of the thinnest on the government payroll. Out of both habit and necessity he lived a Spartan lifestyle that even other teachers he worked with found disconcerting – not that Walter Bevan was ever close enough to any of his colleagues for them to know him well.

He developed a reputation as 'the man that lived out of tins'. Tinned milk, tinned corned beef, tinned fish, tinned vegetables, and as an occasional treat, he'd buy himself some tinned beer.

Even so, by the time he launched his foray into University he had little savings from his time as a teacher – not really enough even for his mostly modest requirements. So he was obliged to work as a lecturer, and sometimes, more gallingly, a tutor.

"If it wasn't for the fact that University work, paid better I'd have never bothered with it," he continued to himself, whitewashing in his mind both the intellectual ambition and the financial necessity that had driven the decision.

Drayden stood at the mouth of the cave, eyebrows raised in curiosity. Bevan was oblivious to the look, and continued his musings.

'Admittedly the research, facilities were better,' he thought, reflecting on the positive side of his long career. 'That was the real saving grace. Made it, possible to endure the, blasted know-it-all students.'

It was bad enough that he had to put up with minds less able than his in the faculty. By rights he should have been Dean. He knew he'd only received Senior Lecturer status by sheer longevity. His lack of people skills and undisguised dislike of 'class contact' always worked against him. The professor never regarded those things as important, and his regular loud exposition on that fact was a more effective career blocker than the attitude itself.

But he could give some grudging respect to other members of the staff. They had qualifications. They could substantiate their expertise, even if it didn't match up to his own. Students were another matter. They were supposed to be there to learn, not to try to show off what they thought they already knew.

That was what Bevan really couldn't abide. Students who knew more than he did.

"Thought that they did, anyway. That was it – students, who thought they knew more than me! Wrong of course. They should, respect my authority. That's how, I was raised – to respect authority. And I've worked long and, hard to become that authority. How dare anyone, anyone, not show me enough respect?"

"Now what's wrong?" called Drayden curtly. "You're grumbling to yourself again."

Disturbed from his reverie, Bevan glared at his assistant. "I have an errand for you," he said.

.o0o.

The session in the tavern in Drayden's less than delightful company left a sour taste in the mouth of the five companions that even a good breakfast in the shared kitchen of their rented house couldn't dispel.

Scarlet looked up from scraping out the bottom of her yoghurt container. "If that man is one of the archaeologists that Costelow was talking about I can understand why the locals are upset. He's rather lacking in sensitivity, isn't he?"

Wilko stuffed a forkful of bacon and egg into his mouth so as to not give voice to his immediate response about pots, kettles, and the relative blackness thereof.

John B. was similarly diplomatic, opting to focus on his agreement about Drayden's character as he said, "Imagine a lovely little cottage garden carefully tended by a white haired old lady every day for forty years. Now imagine a runaway goods train jumping its track and plowing through the garden. Drayden is about as sensitive as that train. Less, probably. The goods train wouldn't go back to make sure it hadn't left an azalea standing."

Jazz slid a piece of potato cake around her plate soaking up chilli sauce. She waved her knife thoughtfully as she said, "I just don't believe him."

"Drano? Can't fault your judgement there," agreed John B.

"There's something he's not telling us. I'm sure he must know Harlan, and where he is. Where this 'Cobbemarmoo' place is."

Darren nodded and between mouthfuls of egg-laden toast said, "We haven't seen the name anywhere. Not on road maps, tourist maps, nowhere."

"Right then," said Wilko from the kitchen sink where he's already begun washing up, "I reckon it's time we got serious about finding the place. Something funny's going on."

"Er…" Scarlet began uncertainly, "Robert, I – appreciate your determination to help Jacinta, but I should point out that, allowing for the time we'll need to travel back to Canberra, we're nearly at the end of the leave we've all taken."

"Ah… I suppose we must be," Wilko admitted uncomfortably.

John B. shrugged as he stood up and ambled towards the sink with his empty plate. "My leave's indefinite after… what went on at home." He discreetly avoided mentioning the attempts on his life that had culminated in a bomb blast in his front driveway. "Darren quit his job. How much leave have the two of you got up your sleeves?"

"I have lots, I imagine," replied Scarlet. "I've taken very little."

Stewart nodded "I would have thought that," he said non-committally. "Wilko?"

"I think I've got a fair bit left, but hey, I'll take leave without pay if necessary."

"You guys are bloody incredible," Jazz said appreciatively. "What can I say except thank you? All of you."

"It's what – friends – do," replied Wilko a little self-consciously.

"I'll ring the office and sort it out with Kaiser Ron," offered Stewart.

"Kaiser Ron?" repeated the blonde, puzzled.

"Sorry, nickname. Ron Kaiser – boss to Wilko, Scarlet and me back in Canberra. Anyway, I'll take care of the leave question. Beyond that though, we need a plan," said John B., uncharacteristically the organizer. "Maybe we have a word with this Costelow bloke. He seems to know something about what's going on."

The wizard went to crack his knuckles ominously but was stopped by the plaster on his hand. "Bugger!" he exclaimed. "That's right – I'm supposed to get this cast off my hand today."

Wilko looked at his old friend, somewhat concerned at the ominous overtones of the gesture. It seemed the aggravation that Drayden had provoked hadn't yet worn off. John B. wasn't normally short-tempered but it might be wisest to keep him away from the possible provocations of the firebrand lawyer.

"Good idea about Costelow," agreed the Tasmanian. "I'll find his office and see if I can get in to see him. Make an appointment at least."

"I like the idea of actually getting out and doing something practical. I'll

74

go with you," declared Jazz.

Wilko smiled broadly. "It's gone nine. His office should be open soon, if it's not already. Let me finish clearing up here and we can head off."

"You two get going. I'll finish that," offered Darren. Putting action to his words he walked over and took the scourer pad from Wilko's hand.

John B. raised a wordless eyebrow. This experience was obviously having an effect on all of them – his young housemate normally volunteered to wash dishes only when there was no crockery left in the house that was clean enough to eat off.

Picking up a tea towel Scarlet remarked, "I've been thinking about what young Darren said. The name Cobbemarmoo must appear somewhere, however small the place is. I think the local library might be worth visiting."

"How about I go with you? I don't mind helping with research. I've done plenty setting up game scenarios," offered the young man.

Scarlet looked uncertain. "We-e-ll…"

"It's a good idea, I reckon," said Stewart. 'My young mate's looking for some direction, and he's got a better head on his shoulders than he gets credit for' was his unspoken thought.

Very soon after, John B. stood in the hall of the house, telephoning his boss' office.

The wizard couldn't resist a smile when a familiar female voice came back down the line from Canberra, saying "Ron Kaiser's office. Elizabeth Dance speaking."

"Elizabeth? Hi! John B. Stewart. Is Ron around?"

"No mate – sorry. He's in a meeting. How's the holiday going?"

"It's… ah… having its moments."

"Seeing lots of interesting stuff?"

"Yeah. Yeah, we certainly are." Behind his vague answer lay the thought, 'Like demons and death I'm very glad you were spared'.

Elizabeth caught a trace of tension in his voice. Concerned, she asked, "Is everyone okay? Are you… okay? You did leave Canberra thinking someone was trying to kill you."

"Like you said, pretty lady, lots of interesting stuff. But yeah, we're okay. And I'm okay. Thank you for asking. I'll tell you about it when we get back."

"Sounds good."

"Don't know about good…. But I'm looking forward to the conversation. It'll be delayed for a little while yet, though."

"Trouble?" asked Elizabeth.

"Aah – I hope not. We're trying to help out a friend who's got a problem. Can you let Ron know we want to extend our leave? I'm guessing at least a week, maybe more."

"Sure. If you've got the leave I can't see a problem. It's quiet here at the moment. I'll tee it up with the Kaiser. Who's the friend? Anyone I know?"

John B. smiled. "No, I doubt it. A young lady Wilko's taken a bit of a shine to."

"Our Wilko? I definitely have to hear about this!"

"All in good time, pretty lady. Actually we did encounter someone you might remember. Was Rod, sorry, Roderick Drayden still around when you started?"

"Drano? Yes. Not for long, lucky for me. He was far too full of himself."

Again John B. chuckled. "Your memory serves you well. Time hasn't mellowed him, I'm afraid."

"Well if he's got anything to do with this strife your friend's in, you be careful. I always thought there was something a bit dangerous about that creep."

"He'd probably take that as flattery. It's alright, I'm hoping to have as little to do with him as possible. Sorry mate, this call will be costing me a fortune – I'd better go. I'll let you know when we're heading home as soon as I know. Take care."

"I will. You too. Y'all come back now, y'hear?" she said, putting on the Southern drawl they sometimes affected during their idle flirting.

"Yes ma'am!" was the cheery reply in an appropriately matching accent.

John B.'s smile was just a little wistful as he replaced the telephone handset. He shook his head briskly, as if clearing cobwebs, and went into the lounge to join the others.

"How did it go?" asked Wilko. "Kaiser Ron okay with us extending our leave?"

John B. nodded and said, "He will be, don't worry. He was in a meeting. I left a message with Elizabeth Dance."

"Um – okay. We'll see, I guess," replied the Tasmanian uncertainly. "How's Elizabeth?"

"As lovely as ever, by the sound of her," the wizard replied.

"John! She's a happily married woman!" came a waspish call from across the room.

"I'm well aware of that Scarlet!" replied Stewart equally sharply. "Sometimes, though, I admit that I…"

"Don't you dare wish she wasn't!" snapped Scarlet.

"I wasn't about to! I was going to say, sometimes I admit I wonder about how happy she is, that's all."

"Sorry," was the quiet reply.

Wilko scratched his head. "John's got a point. Her husband Sonny is a bit of a funny bugger."

Jazz snorted with mirth. "Sonny Dance? You couldn't wonder if he was a bit odd with a name like that!"

Stewart walked back out of the room, saying, "Yeah, well, that's a thought for another time. Right now we've all got places to be and things to do. I'm off to the doctor's."

Wilko was too pleased to be walking out with Jazz to notice his friend's abruptness. But as they left the house to walk to the library Scarlet and Darren did exchange looks of faint unease.

Darren shrugged uncertainly. "For another time, he said. Fair enough, I suppose."

"I suppose so," agreed Scarlet, surprised at her own concern.

Nobody noticed Kat pick himself up off the lounge room carpet, stretch, and quietly slip out the open front door. His tail waved as he trotted, unusually briskly, after Wilko and Jazz.

.o0o.

Harlan didn't bother to look again into any of the empty boxes. First glance had been enough to confirm that they were all unencumbered by food or drink.

Only the top box on the pile that Bevan and Drayden had left for him had been full. That was the box that Bevan had kindly levered open for him himself before departing. Indeed, that was the only one that had contained anything except the odd bit of shredded newspaper or dead insect.

The positive thing was that he'd made this discovery before the top box was completely empty – when he'd taken it down to rummage inside and noticed that the box below had shifted rather too easily when bumped.

The negative thing was that it wasn't far off being completely empty. It held three cans of spaghetti and sausages, a small bag of potato chips, and two 1.5 litre bottles of water. The last represented the biggest potential problem – in those weather conditions that was scarcely a day's supply of water.

The Hawaiian stood with hands on hips and considered his options. Means of communication: none. Means of transport: feet. For all practical purposes, none. Food: little. Water: less. Hope: none obvious. Faith: abundant. Something would sort itself out. Or not. Fretting wouldn't change things either way.

'I'm better off occupying my mind with the task at hand,' he mused.

'Be sensible: don't over-exert physically, do what I can to make these provisions last, stay busy, and wait.'

"Mana… mana… all power comes from within, nothing happens to me without my participation…" Hunter closed his eyes and inhaled deeply, held the breath, then let it out slowly.

"Alright then," he said to himself. "Meditation comes later. First, make a condensation trap so I can collect some water overnight. Then…" He looked around the site with eyes still bright with fascination. "Then I've got drawings to do, notes to write, and things to ponder. Questions to ask – good questions, at that!"

With a cheery whistle that would have bemused most observers of his plight, and which would have certainly irritated the hell out of the man nicknamed Drano, Harlan set about assembling the components of a simple apparatus to harvest a small amount of life-preserving water.

'It may not be the final answer,' he mused, 'but it will delay the final question.'

.o0o.

11 THE 98% OF LAWYERS

Wilko had been quite surprised to find no receptionist in attendance at Carl Costelow's office.

In truth, there were a number of reasons for this apparent inefficiency on the lawyer's part.

For one thing, the practice didn't really do enough business to justify the expense. Far more of his time was spent on Activism (i.e. maintaining a profile in the national media which enabled him to charge like a wounded bull for both written articles and personal appearances) than on his actual profession.

Fortunately for Carl, money wasn't really a problem for him. His family had been generous in providing the means to keep him in business, especially when that business was in a distant part of the country.

His father in Melbourne came from what is called 'old money'. So too did his mother's father, although his maternal grandmother had been an aboriginal girl fostered to the wealthy family. She was the source of the Aboriginality of which he was so publicly proud. Her heritage had been handy at Law School too, when he'd been able to claim "Discrimination!" whenever threatened with failure.

A receptionist wasn't really necessary, he'd finally decided. With the aid of his trusty answering machine Costelow could manage his own phone calls, and he was more than verbose enough to prepare his own correspondence. He even knew how to make his own coffee.

Furthermore, staff proved hard for him to get and to keep. When it came right down to it, Carl Costelow was not a nice man to work for. A handful had tried, and learned that the hard way. Word got around in a place the size of Alice Springs.

There are benefits in that sort of 'network' too, of course, and in his earlier days of establishing his 'credibility' with his 'tribal brothers' he had taken advantage of it.

His favourite ploy for ingratiating himself with certain people had been to find a way around strict laws prohibiting the sale of alcohol on Aboriginal Reserves – government nominated "tribal communities". Carl bought a dilapidated old car with a very large boot capacity.

He would drive the car out to one of the isolated communities and 'sell' it to someone there for a few hundred dollars. Upon purchase, the new owner would seem to be surprised and delighted at finding that the car boot was packed with cartons of beer and bottles of rum. The treasure trove removed, Carl would buy the car back for twenty dollars and drive away, all parties content with the transactions.

He was a lawyer. He knew what was legal. Ethical was a different matter, especially given the problems that alcohol was known to cause on some of those isolated communities. The tribal elders and councils in several had been among the leading proponents of the laws limiting or prohibiting sales.

But ethics weren't Carl's strong point.

An open door in the empty reception area led into the comfortable room that was what Costelow considered the 'nerve centre' of his operation. The lawyer had been at his desk, engrossed (ironically as it happened) in searching for information on his computer about Professor Walter Bevan.

Looking up at the sound of someone's entry he called out, "Yes? What do you want?"

"Good morning, sir," replied Wilko at his diplomatic best. "We're looking for information from a man with local knowledge, and I hear that you're the best."

Out of the lawyer's line of sight Jazz rolled her eyes and muttered, "You don't half lay it on with a bloody trowel, do you?"

"Only when I need to," was the whispered reply.

His ego stroked and his curiosity piqued, Costelow called them into his room. The front door was left half open.

Walter Bevan, or indeed John B. Stewart, might have asked, "When is a door not a door? When it is ajar."

Better for everyone then that neither of those two was nearby at that moment. Who was nearby was Kat. The big Persian had unobtrusively followed the pair all the way from the house. Now he quietly slipped past the door that was ajar and stood, head tilted to one side, apparently listening to the conversation in the inner office.

Wilko and Jazz had outlined to the lawyer the reasons for their visit.

"So you're not locals then. I didn't think I recognized your faces," mused Costelow.

"No, we're staying at a guesthouse over on Mutumutu Street. Does that matter?" asked Jazz in growing impatience.

"Merely an observation," was the airy response.

While they spoke there was a rhythmic whirr in the background as the printer attached to Costelow's computer produced page after page of information. Wilko and Jazz decided it wasn't worth getting the lawyer offside by indulging their curiosity. So they concentrated on their questions rather than watching the paper piling up on the floor behind Costelow.

Kat quietly padded into the room and over to the growing mound of papers. He sat and watched the printer's output for a minute or two, his head tilted on one side. Then he reached out a paw, pulled several sheets off the pile, gently picked them up in his mouth and silently slipped back out the front door of the office without being noticed.

Meanwhile Costelow was saying with only faint diplomacy, "I repeat that I really have only the roughest idea of where the archaeological team is. They are somewhere in the ranges north of us."

Jazz curled her lip and said "Aren't you the man who was calling on 'your people' to 'drive the invaders out' a few days ago? How do you figure on doing that if you don't know where they are? Come on mate, you must have some idea!"

"Er – no," the lawyer replied, momentarily discomfited. "I'm creating an environment, young lady – an environment for active and positive change."

Wilko frowned. "With respect, Mr. Costelow, what you're doing is encouraging violence."

The activist went on the attack. "That's a typical white reaction! Automatically you expect the worst of me and my people!"

"Hang on just a minute…" Wilko began to protest, but Costelow cut him off.

"I've told you what I can – now I'll ask you to get out of my office."

Jazz fumed "But we…"

"I'm a lawyer by profession. I only ask once," snapped Costelow, now standing, fists clenched belligerently but propped on his desktop.

"But we…"

This time it was Wilko who interrupted the engineer, saying, "We don't butt heads with lawyers." He turned back to Costelow. "We've asked. You've answered. Thank you." Taking Jazz gently but firmly by the arm he led the way out of the office.

The English girl made a point of slamming the front door shut as she left.

It was only after the echoes of the slamming door faded behind his uninvited visitors that Carl Costelow allowed a look of concern to cross his face. He sat back down at his desk. After a moment or two of twirling a pencil in his fingers he remembered the file he'd been printing when Wilko and Jazz had arrived.

He picked up the papers from the printer tray and where they'd spilled on the floor and started sorting them into order. As he did he realized, with considerable surprise, that several pages were missing.

"Now, how the hell did they do that?" he wondered aloud to himself. He frowned. He tapped at his desk with the pencil, twirled it a few more times, then reached for the phone. He hit one of his speed-dial numbers.

The number belonged to a telephone in a house in a much rougher part of town. When that phone rang it was answered by a thirty-something aboriginal man, heavily bearded and heavily paunched.

"Murph's place," he said when he picked up the receiver.

"Put Murphy on," ordered Costelow.

"Can't. He's not here."

The lawyer closed his eyes momentarily and sighed before continuing, "Hello Burgstetter. It's Carl Costelow here."

"Hello Mr. Costelow." There was a silence. "Did you want something?"

The lawyer twirled his pencil in irritation. "Yes, Burgstetter, I did. I wanted to speak to Murphy."

"Can't. He's not here."

"So you said. Will he be back soon?"

"Dunno. He's out on his bike."

"Right, okay… Look, Burg, you're Murphy's adjutant, aren't you?"

"Eh?"

"Number Two man in the Mob? You are, aren't you?"

"Yep. That's right," replied the big man. The pride in his voice was audible.

Costelow couldn't repress a smile as he imagined Burgstetter's chest swelling over his ample stomach. "Okay Burg," he replied, "I want you to pass on a message to Murphy for me."

"Right." There was another pause. "You going to tell me the message, Mr. Costelow?"

"Eh? Oh, yes. I've just had a visit from a young woman…"

"That sounds good!"

"Eh?" The lawyer sighed again. "I see. No, Burg, it's not especially good. She's annoying, pushy, cleverer than I'd like, it seems, and just might cause me problems in the future."

"Ah. That's not so good."

"No indeed. I can't put my finger on why, but I've a feeling there's trouble ahead."

"Murph's Mob – we're good at trouble!"

"Yes Burg, I know that," Costelow replied. 'That's why I pay you,' he thought but didn't say aloud. Instead he said, "I just don't want this woman getting in my way, alright?"

"Right."

"She's new in town. Staying over on Mutumutu Street…" Abruptly there was another knock on the door of the office. One of the lawyer's few but lucrative clients had dropped by. Putting his hand over the mouthpiece of the phone Costelow called to the newcomer, "Just a moment – be right with you!"

Returning his attention to Burgstetter he continued, "I'll have to make this quick. She's a white woman, quite attractive in her own way, I suppose. Pick her up and hold onto her there at the Mob's place while I… chase something up. Oh, and you better get the white fellow who's with her, too, just to be on the safe side. There's not much of him so he shouldn't give you any difficulties. Have you got all that?"

"Yep. What do you want us to do with them once we've picked them up?"

"Just hold onto them until I say so. It shouldn't be long. I'll make sure there's no trouble for you and the Mob," he lied smoothly. "Now I must go."

"Bye, Mr. Costelow," said Burgstetter to a phone which had already been hung up.

*

Walking along a street shaded by eucalypts, Jazz was still fuming with impotent rage.

"That bastard! I'm bloody sure he knows more than he told us," she said, just keeping her voice below shouting level.

"Probably, probably," said Wilko, nodding. "Or maybe not."

She stopped in her tracks. "Eh? What's that supposed to mean?"

"He might genuinely not know anything. He might just be winding us up. Being a bastard just because he can. Part of that 98% of lawyers that give the rest a bad name."

Jazz thought about that for a moment then smiled. "I'm bloody glad I'm an engineer and not a lawyer."

Wilko smiled back. "Me too. Listen, that went quicker than we figured. Can I buy you a coffee before we go back to the house?"

"No," was the quick reply.

The Tasmanian's face fell. Jazz grinned at the look he'd failed to hide and playfully linked arms with him.

"But you can shout me a cup of tea!" she said.

.oOo.

Roderick Drayden was, in a way, torn by indecision. It was an unusual situation for a man who was in the habit of seeing the world in simple terms: basically, he was right and everyone else was wrong, only they were too stupid to know it.

It probably wouldn't have comforted him to consider that his mentor Professor Bevan had a broadly similar world view. Perhaps that was what had drawn the two men together as unlikely allies – they despised each other less than anyone else they knew.

Such introspective musings were not on Drayden's mind this morning, though. He was back in Alice Springs to run the 'errand' Bevan had given him. And there was the conflict. He didn't want to be back in town. He liked either isolation, or somewhere so big and crowded that it was easy to not be noticed. When Roderick Drayden wanted to be noticed, he wanted it to be on his terms and for his own purposes.

Conversely though, Drayden didn't want to be at Cobbemarmoo either. Perhaps it was an after-effect of the little 'time off' he'd given himself at the tavern the day before, but he was just finding the Professor even more irritating than usual this morning.

Mad old bugger. The stuff they were working on could make their names and their fortunes. Write it up interestingly, propose some really outrageous suggestions and theories without quite committing to anything

– some publishers ate that sort of thing up, and so did a good chunk of the public. The paying public. There could be a best-seller in this. That meant nothing to Bevan though. They had enough material to do something with – the stubborn old man was becoming a liability. 'He doesn't see the bigger picture,' mused Drayden to himself.

He was entirely wrong, of course. It was just that Walter Bevan saw a very different, and much bigger 'bigger picture'.

But now here he was, back in bloody Alice bloody Springs again. The errand made sense, he admitted that. They wanted Hunter's girlfriend distracted, deflected, taken out of the picture.

Had she been alone they would have had no qualms about helpfully driving her out to where the Hawaiian had been abandoned then leaving her to share his fate. Two could quietly die of thirst and starvation as readily as one. The presence of the rest of the motley crew complicated that.

Drayden grudgingly admired Bevan's plan. The Professor had ground up a combination of several of the different tablets he took for various age-related ailments like arthritis and high blood pressure. He had then carefully wrapped the powder in plain white paper and given it to his protégé.

Drayden's errand was to take the drugs to the local police, explaining that he'd been approached in the tavern by the English lass and her companions and offered a choice of illegal substances. He'd made this small purchase as a responsible citizen so as to ensure there would be evidence against the villains.

The charge might or might not stick, but it would surely be a major inconvenience and distraction. It would have the further benefit of undermining her credibility if she tried to make trouble about her missing boyfriend.

When the archaeologist arrived at the police station he first met with Sergeant Conroy – the officer in charge.

Conroy was a career copper, for all the right reasons. He had a deeply ingrained sense of duty and a real commitment to his community that far outweighed any ambitions he might have had to move on to more glamorous postings. There was a certain world-weariness about him, but it would be a mistake to think he was 'a bit slow' as people sometimes did, to their cost.

The archaeologist was well into his carefully laid out story. Conroy had said little. He had just nodded occasionally and apparently made mental notes. Drayden couldn't read the expression on the sergeant's face, but he wasn't sure if he was getting through.

Suddenly the phone on the desk rang. It was the sergeant's direct line, not the generally used station number.

The policeman held up a hand to interrupt Drayden then picked up the receiver.

"Conroy. Yes?"

Drayden strained his ears inquisitively but was unable to make out the caller's words.

Conroy closed his eyes and sighed quietly. "Yes. Yes, absolutely, Councillor. I'll send one of my men now, ma'am. What?"

The sergeant rubbed his forehead in silent irritation. "No, of course. Yes, I can deal with it myself. What – right away? Yes Councillor, if you insist. You do, yes… I'll be there as quickly as I can."

Drayden failed to suppress a smile at Conroy's obvious aggravation.

The policeman glared at the phone. "I swear some of these people think we're their own private security firm. I'm sorry, Mr. Drayden, I have to dash off. I'll get my senior constable in to talk to you."

Conroy quickly suited action to the words. As he left the station he said to his designated right hand man, "Serge, there's a bloke in my office. His name's Drayden. Got some story about being sold drugs in the Tavern by some people he used to know over east. Look after it."

Serge Steinmetz was a completely different specimen of career policeman. To put it bluntly, he was a bully. Dressing him up in a uniform only made it harder for people to stand up to his thuggery. He was the big blonde Viking type who had been at the centre of the confrontation that had broken out at Costelow's rally.

"Right, Sarge," Steinmetz rumbled, and swaggered into the office.

Drayden started to repeat his story with considerable irritation at first, but as he went on he surprised himself by relaxing a little. Serge Steinmetz was no academic – he sometimes spelt his own name wrong – but he and Roderick at some primal level recognized in each other kindred spirits.

Both were athletes obsessive about a solitary discipline: body building and long distance running respectively. Both shared a belief in their own superiority to the people around them, and resentment that they didn't receive the recognition they deserved. And both were fundamentally nasty, mean-spirited men.

The constable nodded with satisfaction as Drayden handed over the 'evidence' then asked, "So it's Mutumutu Street they're living on?"

"Yeah, I'm sure that was the name I heard."

"Right, I reckon I know which house it'll be. There's only one guest house there big enough for a group. Give me some names."

Drayden frowned. He'd paid so little real attention to everyone in the Tavern that he couldn't remember the names of any of those he hadn't worked with.

Steinmetz noticed the thin man's hesitation. "Who was it invited you into the pub?" he prompted.

"Robert Wilkes. Short bloke. Light brown hair, cut a bit shorter than mine. Carrying too much weight." As far as Roderick Drayden was concerned, almost everyone except himself carried too much weight. "The blonde girl with them – she was the one who actually sold me the stuff. I reckon she's probably the brains of the outfit." Drayden's smooth lie carried a note of reluctance to admit that there might be any brains amongst the group at all, but he realised the girl was to be the main target of the ploy.

"Alright. You come with me, to identify them?" asked Steinmetz.

"Ah… no, I can't just now. They might not be home right now anyway, and I've got to get back to work. I can drop back in later?"

Serge nodded. "Fair enough. Do the paperwork then. I'll get over to Mutumutu Street and see if I can find 'em. Get 'em off the streets."

"Quite right," agreed Drayden, getting up to leave.

The two men shook hands, the archaeologist trying but failing to match the strength of the policeman's grip. Steinmetz smiled at his little triumph as the runner left the station. The unpleasant smile broadened further as he contemplated the task ahead of him.

Serge liked giving out-of-towners a hard time. Easier pickings than some of the local hard cases, like that damned Murphy. Bloody biker and his mates had that lawyer on their side too.

Visitors didn't usually get much help from Carl Costelow. Or help from anyone else, for that matter. He figured he was pretty much untouchable on his turf. The constable had to be a bit careful around the sergeant, but he'd be moving on someday, surely, and then it really would be Big Serge Steinmetz's town.

.o0o.

John B. Stewart had spent far too long a quiet uneventful time in the waiting room of Doctor Margaret Jones.

His luck at getting to see Dr. Jones immediately and without an appointment when they'd first arrived in Alice Springs turned out to have been an aberration. Normal practice was now resumed.

It had perhaps been overly optimistic, he supposed, to turn up slightly before the time of his appointment. Experience in other medical establishments had shown though, that arriving late never seemed to make any difference to the actual waiting time.

Odd, that. If you arrived on time for a 10.30 appointment, you'd perhaps get to see the doctor by 11.30. Maybe 11.15 if fortune smiled upon you. Try getting there at 11.00 for your 10.30 appointment, and you shouldn't expect attention before the afternoon.

The waiting room television offered no comforting distraction, the receptionist having determined that she wanted to keep one eye on the Home Shopping Channel, no matter what the preferences of anyone else in the room.

Amongst the plethora of outdated women's magazines in the rack – some so old that Kylie and Jason's love lives were still a hot topic – John B. had managed to find two back issues of National Geographic. They were if anything older than the other magazines, but excellent photography and intelligent discourse date less quickly than fashion and 'celebrity'.

Even so, Stewart found himself making an effort to read very slowly to have his distraction stretch as far as possible. Despite that, after devoting more attention to the advertisements than he normally would, he was rereading articles that had particularly caught his interest first time around.

Nodding thoughtfully at an article on the fast-diminishing forests of Madagascar he was just in the process of saying to himself, "Now there's a place I really must visit someday," when Dr. Jones came to the door of the waiting room.

"Mr. Stewart?" she called.

John B. looked up at her and smiled as he got, rather stiffly, to his feet. The doctor returned his smile and led him into her consulting room. Something that might have been a snarl flitted across the face of the receptionist as he passed.

After carefully cutting off the plaster cast Dr. Jones was gently pressing the damaged area of the wizard's hand. Not for the first time she looked quite intently at the face of her patient.

"Do I… know you from somewhere?" she asked, somewhat self-consciously. She was a pretty woman, with long brunette hair and a complexion that had thus far managed to avoid being damaged by the Outback sun, although it was certainly the type to be vulnerable.

John B. smiled at her as she worked, wordlessly wincing at the sharp jabs of pain. The two looked to be about the same age.

"Probably not. I think I've just got that sort of face," he suggested. "I'm not from round here."

"Yes – I saw the Canberra address on your file. We don't get a lot of Canberrans up here."

"I was a Queenslander before that," John B. acknowledged.

"Really? I'm from Brisbane! I got my degree at Queensland Uni. Could we have met there?"

The wizard nodded. "That might have been it. My memory of Uni days is a bit blurry. Mea culpa – too fond of a drink."

The doctor's smiled faded a little. "I see too much of that around here. I hope you're taking better care of yourself now."

Stewart nodded, not entirely convincingly, as she slipped a blood pressure sleeve onto his arm. "I'm trying to," he said.

"Sounds like you could do with someone to take care of you," Dr. Jones observed.

As the sphygmomanometer sleeve around his arm inflated John B.'s mind wandered back to that morning's phone call. Elizabeth had sounded genuinely worried, and her instincts usually seemed pretty good. Except when it came to choosing a husband, he reflected.

Dr. Jones jotted down the results. "Have you got a history of high blood pressure?" she asked mildly as she started to carefully wind a pressure bandage around where the cast had been.

"No – far from it!"

"Well, it's up a bit now. Not too major, but I'd put it on the high side of normal, and if that's not usual for you – well – just be a bit careful. Your hand isn't healing as well as either of us would like. I think what you need is peace and quiet."

Stewart gave a short laugh and said, "I wish I could get a little bit of peace and quiet!" Then he bit his tongue and looked worried.

Puzzled at the sudden reaction, the doctor asked, "What's wrong?"

"I think I just said a really stupid thing."

"Nonsense, I meant it. Peace and quiet is exactly what you need. I think we could all do with more of that, frankly."

John B. gave her what was meant to be a reassuring smile, which didn't fool either of them, and said, "Peace, yes. I don't think I want it too quiet. And as to your other point, maybe you're right. We could all do with someone to look after us properly. Even doctors."

"Thanks," she said genuinely. "I manage, even all the way out here. If you're still here in a week, come back and see me. Or if you're home see your own doctor."

"I don't actually have a regular doctor in Canberra," he admitted, thinking to himself, 'Though if I'd met one like you I might have'.

As he stood to leave, the wizard held out his good hand, which she took a firm but gentle grasp of.

"I wish you happiness," said John B.

"I've got that," Dr. Jones replied with a little laugh.

Returning the laugh Stewart answered, "I'm really glad."

He was still smiling as he walked back towards Mutumutu Street, even as a small part of his mind fretted over the possible implications of too much peace and quiet.

.oOo.

While John B. was absorbed in his slow perusal of the National Geographic Society's offerings of 1985, Scarlet and Darren were busy gathering such small fragments of information about Cobbemarmoo as they could find in the library.

Acting according to her nature and habit, Scarlet had immediately gravitated towards books and journals. She had started by skimming modern materials and was gradually working backwards through a range of historical papers.

Darren had started out with what he'd hoped would be the shrewd ploy of asking the library staff. Good idea as it was, it proved fruitless as the Head Librarian was a woman from Piraeus in Greece who had only been in Alice Springs for a few months, and her only assistant that day was an Aboriginal girl who came from western Victoria and had approximately no local knowledge either.

With a polite "Thanks anyway" and a shrug of his bony shoulders, the young man had sat down at a computer terminal and typed 'Cobbemarmoo' into a search engine.

There hadn't been many useful results. He'd managed to work out a rough translation – "demon spirit of the water" – or maybe it could be "old" or "ancestor spirit" – but it seemed the name had never been officially applied to a specific place. He'd found a small number of passing references, and by doing searches on other things mentioned in those references had managed to assemble a small list of information.

He sat at a table alongside Scarlet to compare notes. A fair proportion of Darren's notes directed them to the same documents that Scarlet had identified – a fact which quietly impressed her having given no real credence to his research skills – but there were also references to a smattering of other material. Most of that material they were able to find in seldom-opened library drawers, with occasional disinterested aid from the 'assistant'.

The Victorian girl didn't share her boss's enthusiasm for library work, and frankly had little interest in indigenous culture pre-2006. Working in the library was a steady job with a regular income that had got her away from a fading rural township to the comparative 'big smoke' of Alice Springs. With time, luck and persistence she could move on to somewhere on the coast where she was sure life was more exciting. Helping library customers had to be done, sure, but jeez – it wasn't like you were expected to be enthusiastic about it, was it?

Back at their table, the unlikely research colleagues closed the last of their meagre collection of material. Scarlet scribbled final notes in one of the pocket notebooks she habitually carried.

"Well, we know a little bit of 'what', but not much more of 'where' I reckon," observed Darren.

Scarlet nodded and said, "Well put. Somewhere in the MacDonnell

Ranges, which we already knew, but apparently not on a peak."

"In the area of the ranges, not past them. I suppose that's something."

"Mm," she agreed, taking off her glasses to polish them lightly on a tissue. "To be honest, I'm a little troubled by the 'what'. Nothing I can put my finger on beyond the 'demon' reference in the name itself, but there seems to be an undercurrent of – I don't know – warning perhaps, in the traces of oral tradition we've found documented."

"Like there's a reason nobody talks about the place. Like nobody's meant to find it?"

The redhead looked up at her tall companion. "Very good, Darren. I think that's what I'm feeling."

The young man looked concerned. "Doesn't sound good, does it? I hope Jazz's boyfriend isn't mixed up in anything weird like, well, like that business we found in South Australia."

Scarlet's complexion lost some of its colour.

"Don't even think that," she said with a shudder.

Darren scratched at his chin, where a faint discolouration indicated his thus far disappointing efforts to grow a beard. "I wonder if that Old Black Guy could tell us anything," he mused.

"Maybe. There seemed to be a lot to him, didn't there? If he could tell us though, I wonder if he would?"

"He might tell John. They seemed to get on."

Standing decisively, Scarlet declared, "That's another good idea. It did almost seem like they knew each other from somewhere, didn't it? John should be home from the doctor's by now. Let's go talk to him, then look for the old chap."

*

They'd had some discussion about stopping for some lunch on the way home. It was certainly late enough for it. More than enough, as Darren had observed.

They'd gone so far as to stop and look into a couple of fast-food stores as they walked home.

As they beat a hasty retreat from the doorway of one shop where even a rudimentary sense of smell indicated that the oil in the deep fryer had been used several times too often Scarlet observed, "I really don't know how you could stand to work in a place like that!"

"I didn't. I worked in a pizza place," Darren replied mildly. "And to be fair to them, they were pretty strict about hygiene and food quality."

"Hmph. I think the word 'quality' comes down to a matter of opinion."

"It usually does, doesn't it?"

Not for the first time that trip, nor indeed that day, Scarlet looked at the youth with growing respect. There was more to Darren Bond than his unprepossessing, still slightly spotty appearance might indicate. How many hidden depths in how many other people had she failed to notice, she wondered.

"It's not like it's a career," he continued. "But it paid the rent. I guess I'll find something else like it when we get back."

Scarlet resisted the urge to wonder aloud how much rent he could possibly be paying to live in a makeshift cavern walled with books and old blankets under the dining table in John B. Stewart's one bedroom cottage.

Accepting that it was probably just a turn of phrase, she instead asked, "Couldn't you look for something – better?"

"Ah, it's not so bad I guess. People have to eat, so I'm doing something useful."

"You're capable of more. I'm sure your school should have prepared you better."

Darren shrugged. "Maybe. I left early. I was bored."

"Now that sounds like something John Stewart would say!" she replied with some acid.

"Yep. And there's nothing wrong with that."

Even Scarlet caught the hard defensive edge under the placid voice. They continued their walk in silence for a little while, both deep in their own thoughts.

As they turned to enter Mutumutu Street neither was particularly alert to the low rumble of motorcycle engines a little distance ahead of them.

106

Murph's Mob had been approaching the street and had collectively slowed down at the sight of unfamiliar figures – obvious out-of-towners.

Murph leaned over to address the man who'd been grandiosely described as his adjutant. "You're sure about the description, Burg?"

The big man's brow creased in concentration before he nodded. "Yep. White woman, pushy, 'quite attractive' Mr. Costelow said. And he said there wasn't much of the bloke with her."

Murph nodded towards the two walking along the footpath. "Well, he's about as skinny as a starvin' dingo. And she's a bit alright, but I always reckon red haired women can give you a run for your money. Worth the fight, but!"

Burg and a couple of other Mob members looked dubiously at their leader. Clearly in this regard they didn't necessarily share his opinions. Or at least his taste in women. They knew better than to argue, though.

Murph smiled his broad gap-toothed smile. "Yeah, I reckon that's them. Geezer and Curls, you've got the sidecars. You go round the block, pick 'em up from behind. We'll prop in front of 'em in case they manage to make a run for it."

Curls, whose head had long ago been shaved bald and tattooed with an Australian flag barely visible against his brown skin, nodded. "Do we kayo them, boss?" he asked.

The 'boss' looked thoughtful. "Costelow didn't say anything about not hurting them, did he Burg?"

The burly lieutenant shook his head slowly.

"Right then. But… he didn't say we had to hurt them, neither, so… don't knock 'em around unless you have to. Just grab 'em, chuck 'em in the carts, and we'll take off back to the clubhouse toot sweet."

"What?" asked the baby-faced youngest member of the Mob, inevitably nicknamed Geezer.

"It's French," explained Murph patiently. "It means we go real quick."

"Ah. Right. Okay," said Geezer, and together with his best mate Curls, took off to do a quick lap round the block.

As it turned out Murph's simple plan worked quite well. The element of surprise worked in Curls and Geezer's favour. They mounted their bikes onto the footpath and accelerated.

The leading edge of Curls' sidecar caught the back of Darren's long legs squarely. The young man's bony backside landed neatly on the tattered leather seat, all four limbs draped awkwardly over the outside of the cart.

Simultaneously Geezer slowed only a little to throw a long arm around Scarlet's waist as he passed her. Releasing his handlebars for a moment he flung her across his body and managed to deposit her with reasonable accuracy into his sidecar. The woman's flailing arm caught him a glancing blow, but a small split to his lip didn't diminish his pride at the smooth execution of his boss's plan.

It was lessened somewhat though when she swung a small backhanded fist at him quite deliberately and, more by luck than design, managed to catch the same spot on his lip and significantly increase the size of the split.

'Murph was right about bloody redheads wanting to fight,' he thought. Still, Geezer gave his leader an enthusiastic thumbs up as he passed.

"Toot sweet!" called the youngest biker as Murph passed him and the Mob fell in behind to make their rapid way home.

Stunned as they were, both Darren and Scarlet still knew enough to not make any suicidal attempts to jump out of their uncomfortable carriages at high speed. All they could do was be angry and very, very confused.

.oOo.

15 CAT NOT LITTERING

Several of the good citizens of Alice Springs were bemused to see a large white Persian cat walking along the footpath, tail waving like a large furry serpent, clutching in his mouth a sheaf of printed A4 pages.

One inquisitive pedestrian made the mistake of attempting to grab the papers. The incautious fellow soon after presented himself at the rooms of Dr. Margaret Jones to have several stitches inserted into the wounds on his hand.

Having made quite good time getting home, resisting several distractions which might have been food or playthings, Kat was somewhat irked to find the door of the house at Mutumutu Street closed.

No longer waving, his long tail now flicked from side to side in irritation.

Still clutching the papers in his mouth he proceeded to walk a lap of the house, assessing which windows were open.

He recognised the open window of the room shared by John B. and Darren. It didn't require a feline standard sense of smell to pick up the scent of young Mr. Bond's socks. These aromatically disturbing items were airing, or at least affecting the air on the end of the young man's bed, right by the window. Unfortunately, the rest of the household insisted that the bedroom door be kept closed so the odour was less obvious in the communal living areas. A round door handle - the wrong type to be easily operated by paws. No useful access there, then.

Lounge room. Window closed. Move on.

Jazz and Scarlet's room. Again, easily recognised by the scent – not perfume, but lingering traces of incense. Kat gave a small sneeze, leaving an unfortunate stain pattern on the top sheet of paper he still held. Another closed door.

Bathroom louvres.   A tight fit, but manageable. A drop into the shower cubicle, with a glass door that could be pushed open. But the bathroom door may or may not be open, depending on who was there last. Risky. Can always come back to this one if necessary.

Kitchen. Sash window open but barely an inch or two. When he was younger maybe. The tail flicked again. Alright, much younger.

Wilko's bedroom. A room of his own so his loud and creative snoring might be shut in with him every night. Better that than have anyone else lie for hours staring into the darkness, wondering what sound might come next. John B., Darren and Scarlet had already had that experience during the trip and were in no hurry to repeat it. But during the day, the bedroom door stayed open. And the window?

Yes! Enough for some flow-through ventilation. And enough for a determined cat. A casual observer might not have thought so, but at least some of Kat's apparently generous circumference was fur, and he was very, very determined.

A quick jump onto the window sill. Front paws in, then squeeze the head through. Push up – shoulders raise the sash a little more – that's better.

Now there's room for the belly. There's a thought, must check to see if there's still food out. Pull the back legs and the tail in. Easy.

Wilko had left a good pair of dark trousers neatly folded on the end of his bed. Kat dutifully went over and scratched himself vigorously so as to leave a coating of his fur as a thank-you for having given him access to the house.

Then he padded into the lounge room and, at last, dropped Costelow's papers onto the floor in front of an armchair.

The big Persian ambled into the kitchen and lapped a big drink of water. He hadn't realised how much the paper had dried his mouth until he'd got rid of it. After several mouthfuls of not-too-stale cat food he gave a long, self-satisfied stretch.

He strolled back to the lounge, curled up on the little pile of pages, and fell contentedly asleep.

.o0o.

John B. flexed his newly unplastered hand carefully. The bandages would itch in the Central Australian heat and humidity, but it was a definite improvement. He unlocked the front door and walked into the house with a cheery, "Hi honeys, I'm home!"

He was only mildly surprised when no human voice greeted him.

"Hello little mate," was his reply to the "*Mmmraaaow*" which had been his welcome. John B. was probably the only person to address Kat as 'little' with a straight face.

The wizard parked himself in the chair that Kat lay in front of, leaned forward and scratched between the Persian's ears.

"Nobody else home yet, eh? Well, they all had pretty decent jobs to get done. Wonder if I should go and try to help at the library?"

Kat abruptly stood up and with a sharp "Ekh" stuck a claw into one of the pages he'd been curled up on. He shook his paw to dislodge the paper.

"What have you found to lie on?" wondered Stewart.

He picked up the pages, still warm from Kat's body (not to mention creased) and started to read.

"Biography stuff," he mused aloud. "Walter Bevan, Ph. D. and enough other letters to write a Welsh name. Bevan. Bevan – 'old man Bevan' was who that dropkick Drano said he was working with. No coincidence, surely. ”

Having skimmed the pages he was about to settle into the chair to study them properly. 'Some thinking music,' he decided. He perused the small collection of music that had been left for the entertainment of guest house visitors. A Beatles' Greatest Hits compilation appealed so he pulled the CD from its case, reached over and inserted it into the player.

A few songs later he knew the bare bones of Bevan's life story. A career academic, it seemed. A teacher first, then a University lecturer and Research Fellow. Specialist in ancient civilizations of the Mediterranean and what used to be called the Near East. Too caught up in academia to have ever bothered with a family, it seemed.

"Nothing sinister there," John B. said to his feline friend. "So why is something about him really bothering me?"

Kat, once again curled up at the foot of the chair, only opened a sleepy eye for a moment in response.

'I'll try clearing my thoughts,' pondered John B., at which point Hey Jude began to glide from the speakers. An old favourite, it probably wasn't the ideal song to underpin Stewart's attempts to carefully consider the seemingly innocuous Professor Bevan.

He counted the number of 'na-na-na-na's at the end of the song then gave Kat a puzzled look. "I thought there were more of them than that," he said.

Kat barely bothered to look up as the wizard pushed a button on the CD player to replay the track.

After the fourth replay Stewart scratched his head and muttered, "Weird. I get a different count every time. Is something very metaphysical going on, or am I just having more trouble concentrating than usual?"

"*Mmreh*," was Kat's only reply before he turned his head sharply, ears pricked to look at the front door. Tail waving in concern, the big cat walked down the hall and stood at the door, glaring at its closedness with evident annoyance.

Replaying Hey Jude yet again, Stewart was oblivious.

Bare minutes earlier, Wilko and Jazz had been walking up Mutumutu Street.

Deep in conversation they failed to notice the police patrol car slowly rumbling along the street behind them. In the car was the burly descendant of the Norse, Serge Steinmetz.

Wilko stood to one side in the gateway to let Jazz pass. She smiled at the gesture and looked up at the house.

"That's the Beatles playing," she observed. "I'm sure someone's got Hey Jude on 'repeat'."

Just as the two started to walk up the path, Steinmetz brought his car to a halt in the middle of the street, flung open his door and ran across to them.

He grabbed Wilko's collar in a way that tough British TV policemen of the 1950's would have been proud of and lifted the much smaller man off his feet.

"Robert Wilkes?" he demanded.

"Yeah! Wha…?" spluttered Wilko, struggling to speak as his own shirt choked him.

"Put him down, you great lummox!" demanded Jazz, punching the policeman in a bicep you could break rocks on.

Seemingly obedient, Steinmetz let go of Wilko's collar. The Tasmanian dropped and barely avoided landing in a graceless heap on the ground.

The big constable then drew a handgun from the holster at his side and said, "Right, both of you, in the car. You're nicked."

Wilko's mouth opened and shut but no sound came out – the goldfish impression he was becoming uncomfortably familiar with.

The feisty Jazz was not so speechless. "On what charge?!" she stormed.

"Resisting arrest, for a start," replied Steinmetz with a broad but unpleasant grin. At gunpoint he marched them to his car, and handcuffed them both before bundling them into the back seat.

The police car took off down Mutumutu Street at a much greater speed than it had been previously prowling.

Kat hoisted himself up on his hind legs, leant his forepaws against the door, and gave one loud yowl.

Startled, John B. looked up from the stereo. "Kat? What's up, mate?"

He saw the Persian's unusual posture at the front door and hurried over.

"You want out? What – couldn't be bothered with the window?" he asked genially.

The cat glared at him and made a noise something like, "Nrrnrrng."

"Sorry," apologized the wizard as he opened the door, expecting Kat to dash out into the yard.

Instead the animal simply walked out onto the porch and stood looking up the street, his tail waving.

Puzzled, John B. also walked out and looked in the direction of Kat's gaze. "Don't see anything out of the ordinary," he said with a shrug.

.oOo.

Giving up on the Hey Jude question, John B. settled back into his chair to wait for the rest of the household.

"Maybe catch some of that peace and quiet the doctor ordered, eh? She was nice. You'd have liked her, mate," he observed to Kat while scratching the white furry head.

The Persian responded by dropping full length to the floor, taking his head out of Stewart's reach.

The wizard watched the flicking tail. "What's bothering you?" he asked. "I'm allowed to like attractive brunette women, you know. And it's too early for your dinner."

There was no appreciable feline response.

"You just bored with being cooped up in here all day, mate? Tell you what, when some of the others get back you and I can go for a stroll over to that park."

Kat gave something like a sigh, closed his eyes and went to sleep.

"Or not," conceded John B., who was soon drowsing himself as the CD played out into silence.

He drifted into a dream, or something like it. He was all at sea. No, out on the sea, in a small boat built for one.

The boat was tossing and pitching on a violent sea, so badly that he was forced to cling to the sides to avoid being thrown into the dark waves.

In the distance he could see the cause of the water's agitation. A fiery red glow was reflected against a huge, heavy pall of smoke that filled the night sky.

He had no idea of where he was going. He sensed that he should have been able to work it out by currents and stars, but the choppiness of the sea precluded one and the oily black plumes obscured the other. The only light was the red glow, which even at that range reflected off some of the boat's polished timber.

'Smoke on the water and fire in the sky,' he thought. 'I could drift like this for days, or weeks!'

It wasn't long though – less long than it felt, really – before he jolted back to wakefulness.

After a quick check Stewart realised "Still nobody home. I don't like the feel of this."

He tried calling the library, but a recording of a Greek-accented voice advised him that it was now closed. He didn't hold the line to hear the opening hours.

There was similar frustration in calling Costelow's office. That call took him straight to the answering machine. Costelow's long-winded, self-aggrandizing message only irritated the wizard enough to hang up the phone sharply before leaving any message of his own.

"Only message I'd leave that bugger would suggest something anatomically difficult. Probably wouldn't help matters," he told Kat.

He considered driving over to the two locations, or any other part of Alice Springs that might seem helpful. To his further chagrin though a search of the house revealed that the key to Wilko's Triumph was nowhere to be found.

As he spooned the contents of another tin of food into Kat's plate he mused "Probably still got the key in his pocket. Could I hotwire it? Better not – English electrical system, I'd probably blow my fool hand off."

Walking around Alice Springs seemed a pointless option. He truthfully had no idea where to look. It would be typical if the others arrived home while he was out wandering the streets, then they set out to look for him, they kept missing each other, and the whole situation descended into farce.

So he sat in his chair, looking out the window, watching the shadows lengthen.

"I wish I knew what I'm supposed to do next."

Kat looked up from his plate and gave a quizzical "*Mrrah?*" – not easy through a mouthful of whitebait and sardine in prawn jelly. Especially for a cat who was fond of a feed of fish.

John B. grinned back at him. "Sorry mate – I wasn't really asking you. I wish someone would tell me though."

He turned to look expectantly in the direction of both the telephone and the front door, both of which remained mute.

The wizard shook his head. "I should know better – it's not that predictable. This is not the peace and quiet I wanted. Sometimes, old friend, I wonder if this magic is more of a curse than a blessing."

Kat's "*Mmreh*," was even more muffled this time as he didn't bother to extract his face from the plate.

The shadows continued to lengthen.

.o0o.

The afternoon sun was still strong, even as it slipped towards the horizon. As usual, Drayden had gone for his afternoon run, giving Bevan the opportunity to transcribe by torchlight the latest carvings to be exposed by gradual removal of the cavern's fill.

The professor had returned with his notebook to the shade of a canvas awning and was sorting and cataloguing the most recent finds to be sifted from the deep sands of the cavern floor.

The process of cataloguing summoned up memories of those aspects of University life he'd really loved. The acquisition of knowledge, and, he supposed, the opportunity to apply that knowledge. His mind turned back to some of the tutorial groups he'd been expected to teach. Most of the students didn't dare to challenge him by the time he was a Research Fellow, but occasionally one of them might be rude enough to question one of his interpretations.

That was easily dealt with, of course. It wasn't as if he recognised any other scholar as being more of an authority than he was. There were other kinds of rudeness, too. He remembered his first encounters with Roderick Drayden.

A keen student, he'd thought. Well, perhaps not so much keen as determined. It was as though, having set himself the task of obtaining the qualification, he was not going to allow anyone or anything to prevent that. It was an attitude that the professor respected. He didn't like the former public servant. Walter didn't really like anyone. But Drayden had known his place and worked hard, thus becoming the closest thing Bevan ever had to a 'star pupil'. He still didn't like him though.

Meanwhile as the professor wrote, Drayden ran. He ran in a straight line, up and down dunes and across long-dry creek beds. That had become his routine. He would run in a straight line for an hour, turn around and run straight back so that there would be no chance of losing his way in the desert.

He ran long distances not so much for the pleasure of his own company, but the pleasure of having nobody else's.

Roderick hadn't always been quite so misanthropic. Until he was ten he'd been a gregarious little boy, eager to be around people who'd tell him how clever he was, and how good at sport, and all those things that make a kid feel important.

Then his parents unexpectedly had another child. The arrival of little Tracey meant that Roderick was no longer the single central point of the universe in the Drayden household, and he didn't like that.

No matter how good his exam results, or what team he was picked for, or which races he won, he no longer had their undivided attention. Oh, they still said they were proud of him, and perhaps they were, but that wasn't the point. He'd never had to share anything, least of all attention, and he reacted by very quickly becoming surly and bitter. It rapidly began to change his life.

Roderick took that surliness to the sports field. He was picked less and less often for team games, despite whatever ability he had. This was simply because he wouldn't co-operate with team-mates, or coaches, or referees. 'Does not play well with others' began to appear regularly on his report cards.

The same attitude affected his schoolwork. His exam results remained good, but group exercises became a hardship for anyone unlucky enough to be teamed with him.

All these things were everybody else's fault, of course. They weren't as clever or as fast as him - they were jealous, and they were resentful. Boyish arrogance developed a hard edge as he became surer than ever that the people around him just weren't as good as him.

As young Roderick passed through his teenage years the surliness developed into a full-blown meanness. The friends of his childhood abandoned him, repulsed by his physical and verbal bullying.

Tracey grew up tormented by her big brother, always out of the view of their parents. At six years old she broke her arm. Roderick would shove peanuts down into the plaster cast where she couldn't reach, so her skin would itch terribly.

He would deliberately tread on favourite toys, or steal them then shrug and say, "She must have lost it – you know what she's like."

By the time Mr. and Mrs. Drayden realised their little boy wasn't as wonderful as they'd thought he was, he'd left home with barely a 'good-bye'.

An attempt at living in a group house was brief, argumentative, and an unpleasant experience for all concerned. A tiny serviced apartment in a seedier part of town was all he needed, and easy enough to acquire even on a small income.

Roderick's confidence and skill at exams were enough to get him into the Public Service straight from school. It was a lowly clerical position to begin with, but he'd started young and was bright enough to progress despite his obvious lack of people skills.

A Departmental recruitment drive in Canberra took him to the nation's capital, but by then Drayden was looking elsewhere for his future.

Public Service work meant spending too much time with too many other people. No matter how high the quality of your own work, it would always be dragged down by the incompetent idiots around you. Not that they would be the ones blamed when things went wrong – no matter how hard he tried to ensure it. Any chance of success and prestige, even within that limited environment, was far too dependent on the unpalatable 'them'.

The brief explanation of his move into academia that Roderick had given in the Tavern had been as honest as it was terse.

He had been very good at History in school. He may even have been excellent, at least sometimes. He had realised that there was money in antiquities. Money wasn't really a motivator for him, but he could see the potential for prestige and recognition based on his own research, interpretation and talent.

And archaeology could be arranged to be mostly outdoor work. Outdoors – free from the unwanted company of inferior minds. Minds like Walter Bevan's – a very bright bloke, right enough, but he seemed to be stubbornly resisting seeing the commercial opportunities for this discovery.

Roderick knew it was probably the best chance he'd ever have at the fame he deserved. The best thing about fame was that everyone else knew that you were better than them. Now there was a happy thought to sustain him as he ran.

Bevan barely looked up as the younger archaeologist jogged into their encampment. The older man concentrated on his work as the jogger first wiped himself down with a towel then quickly changed from singlet, running shorts and shoes into his more conventional working clothes. Emerging from his tent Drayden was immediately handed his shovel to move more sand.

After a half hour of shovelling and sifting, the professor called a halt while the billy was boiled. Under their canvas shelter, sweat ran down the faces of Bevan and Drayden and dripped into their mugs of tea.

"I wonder if your little errand this morning has, yet borne fruit?" pondered the older man.

Drayden shrugged. "I don't know. Probably. Like I said when I got back, the big copper I spoke to seemed pretty keen to crack the whip."

"Policeman," corrected Bevan, although not forcefully. "I think 'copper' is a term which, fails to denote the proper, respect for authority. But I think you have, done well. It should only be, as you, said, a matter of time. Speaking of which, consider this. If I have a bow and sixty, arrows, and commencing at exactly noon fire one arrow every minute, at what time will I run, out of arrows?"

"One o'clock obviously – no, wait…"

"Ah-ha. Too quick, dear boy. Twelve fifty-nine," the professor corrected.

"That'll do me," said Drayden flatly, and without looking flung the dregs from his mug behind him.

There was a sudden commotion and loud hissing. A two metre long brown snake that had been curled up peacefully on a rock had taken an unexpected shower in warm tea and sugar. The snake raised its glossy black head and stared at Drayden, who now stood staring back.

Bevan looked up idly from his tea. "Ah. An Oxyuranus microlepidotus. Better known as the inland taipan. Not as common here as in, parts further east but not a great, surprise to encounter one either."

"I'm surprised," replied his younger colleague with feeling.

"Interesting species. Very dangerous, venom you know. Neurotoxic, coagulant, but also haemorrhagic. Three times more toxic than, its cousin the coastal, taipan Oxyuranus scutellatus. Yet, oddly whereas the coastal taipan killed many people I believe that there, are no recorded fatalities attributed to this species."

"Really," said the younger man through gritted teeth. He could feel the sweat seeping from his pores. It was cold.

The professor continued idly. "Indeed. I would posit that this statistic, is merely a reflection of very different human population patterns in the, habitats of the two species. The bite of this particular one is still very likely to kill a, grown man so I, believe."

"Oh," replied Drayden quietly.

"Mm, yes. Before the development of, an antivenin some years ago there were, only two recorded survivors of a taipan bite. An interesting statistic."

This news did nothing to cheer Drayden, who stood transfixed like a rabbit caught in headlights. In truth, the snake was almost certainly at least as frightened as Drayden and would have appreciated nothing more than a quiet escape. But while their gazes were locked it seemed neither was going to move.

Bevan quietly put down his mug and reached into a rucksack by his feet. He withdrew a large pistol and, barely seeming to aim, casually fired a single shot that blew the poor Oxyuranus microlepidotus in two.

Drayden shook himself, blinked, and turned to look at the older man.

Bevan was putting the gun back in his rucksack as he remarked, "My father's old, service revolver. Saw duty in New Guinea."

"You're – ah – good with it. Sir."

"Mmph. In my day, a boy was taught to shoot. Important part, of learning to be a man. All gone now of, course. Going soft," he grumbled, returning to his tea.

Recovering from his shock, Drayden gingerly approached the remains of the snake. He prodded at the taipan's head with the toe of his boot.

"Isn't that interesting?" he asked, to no response. "Jaws wide open – it must have been about to have a go at me when you shot it. It looks surprised," he observed with an unpleasant smile.

"Probably muscle, contraction at the moment of, impact," replied Bevan.

"Oh – death agony." Drayden nodded, still smiling. "That sounds good. Is the poison still dangerous, do you think?"

"Well, the creature is hardly in a, position to bite you. No muscle control to release, the venom. I suppose if you jabbed yourself hard enough with the, fangs it would cause a problem. The toxicity I believe degrades over, time of course but antivenene, which is after all made from, the original poison, is stored for quite long periods. All right, enough chit-chat. We have work, to do."

As he picked up his shovel and went to dig more sand from the cavern, Drayden looked back over his shoulder at the snake's corpse. Bevan gave every appearance of having forgotten the incident already.

Later that evening, the professor sat in his tent wrinkling his brow over his notebook, transcribing symbols onto a sheet of paper with a pencil, erasing them and rewriting them in different sequences and combinations.

In the adjoining tent, carefully protecting himself with thick gloves, Drayden quietly busied himself with the unfortunate taipan's head and a roll of plastic film.

.o0o.

19 MOB RULES

It looked like a pretty ordinary, run-down timber house in the rougher part of town. Not least because it was for the most part a pretty ordinary run-down timber house in the rougher part of town. A few small modifications had been made for the sake of security, like replacing the glass in all of the street-facing windows with various pieces of timber or sheet metal.

That was out of a deep regard for privacy and a distrust of prying eyes, not because of any fear of the neighbours, rough as they may be. No neighbours, even in that part of Alice Springs, were rougher than Murph's Mob.

Inside the house had been made comfortable, if not luxurious. The furniture was old but accommodating. Decorating the walls were pictures of motorcycles and a collection of weapons. A few were traditional Aboriginal weapons like spears and clubs, but most were much more modern. Bladed weapons were clearly popular with the Mob: a pair of cavalry sabres, some Japanese katanas, some in ornate embroidered scabbards, even a batleth – a reproduction of the fearsome Klingon sword designed for the Star Trek series.

The Mob were sitting or standing around in the lounge room, several of them holding cans of beer.

Murph hung up the phone with a look of some annoyance. "Still no answer at Costelow's place. You're sure he didn't ring back while we were out, Pretty Boy?"

Pretty Boy, who predictably had a face that looked like it had been hit with a shovel (actually it had been when he was younger, but it really hadn't worsened his looks much) shrugged. He was the oldest of Murph's Mob, and often content to take more than his share of 'minding the store' when the rest of the gang were out.

"Never rang at all, boss," confirmed the homely biker.

"So we still don't know what we're supposed to do with the two in there," said Murph, indicating a locked room.

"Hold on to 'em I guess. That's what Mr. Costelow said," offered Burg.

The boss wasn't wearing his customary grin. "I reckon I'd be happier if I knew why. It's been a few hours already and we ain't heard a thing. I wonder if they know themselves, eh? Maybe we ought to ask them."

With that, Murph slid back the bolt and opened the door of the hitherto locked room.

Scarlet and Darren were tied securely but not uncomfortably and lying on iron framed single beds that were clean, if you allowed a very loose definition of 'clean'. Certainly not clean enough for Charlotte Burke's satisfaction.

She looked up angrily as some of the Mob members entered the room.

"I demand to know the meaning of this!" she raged.

"Yeah, you said that before. A few times," replied Murph genially.

132

"And you've yet to give me a decent answer."

Murph grinned as he sat down beside her and said, "To tell you the truth Red, I dunno that I've quite got one yet."

"What's that supposed to mean?" asked Darren.

The boss shrugged. "Near as I can make out you two have managed to upset a friend of ours – well, not exactly a friend. More… well… someone we do business with… So we're doing him a bit of a favour and looking after you." As he spoke he idly rested a hand on Scarlet's knee.

"Leave her alone!" shouted Darren.

"Hey, relax, Skinny," laughed Curls. "Anyway, I don't see her puttin' up much of a fight herself!"

Darren wasn't laughing in response. "I don't think Scarlet's the fighting type."

The lady in question wordlessly moved her leg from under Murph's hand.

Curls ran a hand over his tattooed pate. "But you reckon you are?"

Burg grinned and shook his head. "C'mon Curls – look at the kid. Even Geezer could break 'im in half."

Opening mouth without first engaging brain Scarlet snapped, "You haven't seen him with a weapon in his hands. He's surprising."

"Yeah?" said Murph curiously. "How good are ya, Skinny?"

"Bit hard to say, tied up like this, eh?" replied the young man, after a considered pause.

"Reckon you're up to a friendly little blue, do ya?" asked Curls.

Darren shrugged in response.

"What do you reckon, Skinny? You game?" prodded Murph.

Bright crimson, Scarlet tried to protest. "I didn't mean…"

"Yeah, alright," interrupted Darren. "I'm game." He proffered his wrists.

Murph obligingly untied the ropes, and then did the same for Scarlet.

"Now, no doin' anything stupid, eh Red?" he said, smiling broadly at her.

"I don't do stupid things," she replied, finding herself struggling to resist returning the smile. "Darren, on the other hand…" she continued, her voice trailing off as they entered the lounge room and 'Skinny' as he seemed to now be called walked around the walls admiring several weapons close up.

"Some of these are really nice," he said admiringly. "Well looked after, too."

Curls looked slightly uncomfortable at Darren's apparent comfort with some very sharp blades and said, "Since this is a friendly little blue, let's not use the good stuff."

"Right," responded Murph. "You leave the good swords and stuff on the walls."

"Nunchakus?" suggested Darren.

Curls looked at the expression on his boss' face. He was pretty comfortable with the weapon himself, but Murph was wordlessly making it clear that there was only meant to be one nunchakus 'expert' in the Mob.

"Nah. Reckon not," the bald biker said. "There's a few other bits and pieces lyin' around."

So saying, he picked up a kendo stick that had been lying on a bench, and gave it a few experimental swings. A little over three feet long, it was four slats of bamboo tied together with leather cords.

Darren picked up what looked like a samurai sword in an especially ratty scabbard. "Not one of your good katanas, then?" he observed to Murph.

The gang's boss laughed. "Heh, not exactly – take a look."

The young man drew the sword from the scabbard. That was a quicker job than expected – the blade had snapped about ten inches along its length so it was barely the size of the hilt.

Curls spun the kendo stick from hand to hand. "Better find yourself something else, Skinny."

"It's alright – I'll take this." Darren looked carefully at the damaged sword as he tossed the scabbard to the floor. "The proper name for it is a ninjato. Samurais used to keep them after a battle. Developed a whole different technique for fighting with them."

For the first time Curls didn't look quite so confident.

"Knowin' what it's called don't mean ya know how to use it!" called one of the watching Mob.

The bald biker brightened at this piece of encouragement. "It's just a broken sword," he said as he swung the kendo stick in a huge arc at Darren's head.

Both hands on the hilt of the ninjato, with a sharp movement Darren blocked the stick with the back of the blade then held the block for a moment. Curls gave the bamboo sword another mighty swing, this time aiming for the ribs. This time as the stroke was parried with the back of the blade the tip of the kendo stick clattered as it was driven to the floor.

Darren took a step back. "Broken's not the same as useless. I hope you've kept the bamboo in good nick. If there's a crack in it or something I'd hate to shatter it."

"Don't you bloody worry about that!" snapped Curls as he advanced on Darren, this time shortening his swings but putting the strength of his broad shoulders into the clubbing movements.

The ninjato danced in short movements to block and parry. Darren didn't swing the weapon so much as angle it, constantly using the back of the blade for defence.

After several fruitless swings Curls took half a step backward to catch a breath and suddenly Darren was advancing on him, bringing the broken sword down in short hard chops that had no backswing, but struck with surprising force.

The biker had to shift one hand hurriedly for fear of losing his fingers, and while his attention was focused on the hilt end of the stick Darren struck two precisely aimed sharp chopping blows. The first reefed the tip off the kendo stick. The second hit the leather binding a third of the way along the weapon. The severed cord was flung across the room as the bamboo slats sprang apart.

Curls was left standing with a comical look of amazement on his face, staring at four not very helpful sticks which looked a bit like a peculiar bouquet in his hands.

The Mob, and Scarlet, stood similarly bemused. It was Murph who broke the spell by applauding.

"Brother, you're good," he enthused.

Darren nodded graciously. "Sorry about busting your shinai," he said. "I can help you retie the naka-yui if you like. The bit that holds it all together."

The bikers' boss grinned and walked over to clap the youth on the shoulder. "I'll hold you to that!" he replied cheerfully.

Still shaking his head in surprise Curls extended a hand. "Okay Skinny, you know your stuff alright. You coulda taken my paw off then, couldn't ya?"

"A friendly little blue, you reckoned, didn't you?"

The bald biker nodded, and the pair shook hands.

Curls ran a hand over his tattooed scalp, wiping away a sheen of sweat. "Where did you learn to fight like that, anyway?" he asked.

"I've been interested in history and weapons since I was a kid. Then, a couple of years ago, I got taught some sword fighting by a guy named Edmund Mapleton – he was an old mate of my brother, and of John," he added with a quick look to Scarlet. "Nice bloke, but his knees were busted up badly so he couldn't dance around like they do in the movies. He taught me to fence while keeping well grounded. Let the sword do the work, and keep your own movements to just the essentials. No fancy stuff just for the sake of it."

"Good advice," agreed Murph.

"I always thought so," said Darren. "I reckon it works for a ninjato just as well as a rapier."

Geezer approached them.

"Hey Skinny, can you teach me about some of them weapons?" he asked.

Murph's grin broadened. "You wantin' to learn somethin' Geezer? Now that's new! Red, you got a good one here," he said throwing a convivial arm around Scarlet's shoulders.

Scarlet scarcely flinched as she said, "I have not 'got' him. He's not mine. Darren is, well, his own man." For a moment she found herself pondering the new respect she realised was growing.

"Good on 'im," replied Murph. "So, has anybody got you?"

Scarlet's blush was nearly incandescent, and it took her a couple of attempts to finally get out the word "No!"

Murph's grin was unaltered. "Don't understand that. What a waste."

Looking at Scarlet, Darren couldn't resist a chuckle. "You look like Wilko when you do that. You know, that goldfish thing he does…"

She clamped her mouth shut and punched the tall youth on the arm. Hard.

"Ow!" he exclaimed.

"Gotta love redheads," said Murph, as several of the Mob exchanged unconvinced glances.

Curls grinned.

"Look," said Murph. "I really don't wanna tie you up and lock you in again, but a favour owed is a favour owed and we said we'd hold onto you until we heard…"

"Heard what from who, and why?" demanded Scarlet, again.

Murph sighed and scratched his head. "I really don't know why. I mean, I'm starting to see how you could get on someone's wick – before they got to know you, but we still ain't heard nothin'. And I don't wanna say 'who' on account of, well, professional courtesy. If I leave you loose, will you stay here in the house overnight? We heard nothin' by morning, we'll go find some answers."

"Together?" asked Scarlet.

"Yeah. Together." Murph was grinning again.

Darren gave the ninjato a small movement, as if to remind everyone he still held it, and said, "We've got friends out there that'll be really worried about us by now. Can we ring them?"

"More like these two, boss?" queried Pretty Boy. "I mean, I like a fight as much as the next bloke, but…"

"Yeah. Sorry, Skinny, but I don't want your cavalry tryin' to ride to the rescue."

"I don't think they'd…"

"Actually Scarlet, they'd probably try to. John B. certainly would," interrupted Darren.

"Scarlet? That your name?" asked Murph in some surprise.

"It's Charlotte, really," she corrected, not without a little warmth.

The biker boss tilted his head as if turning the name over in his mind before answering, "I think I'll stick with 'Red'. So Red, you can have that room to yourself, and Skinny, you can bunk down with some of the boys. Assuming we can trust youse overnight."

Darren and Charlotte exchanged glances then both nodded.

"Sure you can trust them, boss?" asked Burg with more caution than suspicion.

Murph looked into the eyes of each of his 'captives' in turn then replied, "Yeah. Reckon I can tell honour when I see it."

*

Later that night Murph sat on the edge of the bed that Darren had earlier been tied to. He'd 'dropped in to check that Red was comfortable'. She hadn't objected, and had put down the book he had loaned her to chat more amiably than any of her workmates would have imagined.

Indicating the paperback she said, "I haven't read Thucydides since High School. When you offered me something to read I wasn't expecting a selection of history books. I thought it would be more like a box of Playboy magazines or something. Sorry – was that unfair?"

"Nah. We got a few boxes of stuff like that too. That Peloponnesian War there, that's got some int'resting tactics and things in it."

Scarlet gave her captor a long appraising look. He didn't flinch, but returned her stare with a gap-toothed smile.

Finally she said, "You're not a stupid man, Murphy. Why do you live like this? Are you – I don't know – running away from something?"

He shook his head, the smile unwavering. "I'm just re-e-eal independent."

"You picked up Darren and I when you were ordered to."

"Not ordered. Asked. Like I said, a favour owed is a favour owed. Sometimes some of the boys get into a bit of trouble and we need to ask favours."

"It's never you in a 'bit of trouble' then," Charlotte suggested ironically.

Murph happily ignored the sarcasm. "Almost never. Anything else I can get you?"

With a wry smile of her own Scarlet replied, "I don't expect you've got lemon barley water in the kitchen."

"Got lemon cordial. Curls likes it in vodka. I can offer you some of that."

"The cordial or the vodka?"

"Either. Both if you like."

Thinking back later her own chuckle surprised Charlotte Burke, as did her spontaneous reply, "Not this time."

They looked at each other thoughtfully for a moment.

Scarlet asked cautiously, "So, if you're so independent, why the Mob?"

Murph's gaze was steady. "Independent ain't the same as not belonging. Belonging's a good thing. You oughta try it."

"I don't know that I'm the 'gang' type. I mean – what do you all do all day? Just ride around?"

The first reply was a deep and genuine laugh. Then, "That'd be nice! Nah, a lot of the boys have got real jobs an' such. This is a place to hang out, call home, like I said – belong."

Scarlet nodded. "I see – I think. What sort of jobs? I don't mean to pry, or sound suspicious, but – I'm sorry, you hear so much that's negative about motorcycle clubs…"

"Yeah, I know. But not everyone sells drugs or runs brothels. Most don't.
142

Most of us just want to ride our bikes and keep company of people that dig the same stuff we do. Same as other people – you too, eh?”

“I… um… suppose so.”

“None of the Mob works nine to five stuff. Well, Pretty Boy does a couple of days a week in an office – he’s a tax agent. Some of the boys work Security in one of the nightclubs in town. Geezer does a bit of landscaping – well, laboring for a bloke who’s got a gardening business. Curls is the greenkeeper for one of the bowls clubs.”

“Wow! There’s some surprises there, I must admit.”

The ‘boss’ grinned broadly.

“What about you, Murphy? What do you do, besides be in charge of the Mob?”

“Just Murph. Murphy’s the name on me licence, not the one I use with friends.”

Scarlet blushed as he continued.

“I ride. Always have, since I was a kid. Used to ride speedway for a living – I was pretty good at it, too. Then I got busted up in an accident. That’s how I got this dental work,” he said, pointing to the distinctive gap in his smile.

“Ah. I had wondered if… er…”

“It was in a fight? Heh heh – you’re not the first. I’m happy to let people think that. Good for the image. Pity that wasn’t the only damage I copped. Busted up me ribs, tore up me shoulder, and I got a whole bunch of metal inside me leg holding it together."

Unconsciously Scarlet reached to rest a hand on his leg – a gesture of concern that would have surprised everyone back in the Canberra office. Everyone including the Charlotte Burke who'd worked there only a couple of weeks earlier.

"That sounds painful. I guess that's an understatement, sorry," she said softly.

Murph shrugged. "It wasn't much fun. Got a good compo payout since the accident was the fault of the company that owned the track I was ridin' on. Invested the money pretty good. It'll keep me goin' for a while yet." Scarlet couldn't disguise her look of surprise.

The biker's grin barely dipped. "Like you said, Red – I ain't stupid. You get some sleep, eh? Big day tomorrow I reckon. Tomorrow we try to figure out what you did to get you into all this trouble."

He casually moved her hand off his leg. That startled Scarlet. She'd hardly been aware it was there. She was much more self-conscious about returning his smile, but managed a small wave as he left the room.

As the door closed behind him, she lay back on the bed and thought about unconsidered depths, and about belonging.

.oOo.

John B. was quietly playing yet another CD to try to settle his nerves. He'd tried some classical music but it turned out to be a bit too heavy on blaring brass and crashing cymbals to be soothing. Cheesy covers of show tunes hadn't worked either. He'd finally taken a punt on the slightly ominous-sounding Hollyridge Strings. It was a pleasant surprise to find that the Strings played almost surreal lounge music.

Kat lay stretched out beside the armchair that Stewart occupied and vacated like a fiddler's elbow. The Persian appeared to be asleep but he was actually on the same high alert as his purple-shirted friend – he just preserved his energy better.

The last of the twilight was fading. Yet again Stewart went to the door, opened it, looked up and down Mutumutu Street, then chewed his lip and closed the door again.

With a sigh the wizard wandered back to the chair and slumped into it. Again.

"There's something crook going on in Alice Springs, old mate," he said to the cat. "And somewhere else… out there…"

He waved a hand vaguely towards the desert expanses that surround the town.

Without opening his eyes Kat let out a long low *mmrreooww*.

Raising an eyebrow John B. started to ask ,"What's the matter with…?" when there was a gentle knock at the door.

Stewart almost leapt from the chair in relief, and then stopped suddenly part way across the room.

'They should all have a key, so why knock?' he mused, and so took the last few steps to the door quietly.

He waited a moment. The gentle knock wasn't repeated, but he opened the door anyway.

"G'day brudder!" said Old Black Guy, who smiled and stuck out his bony hand.

Shaking the hand warmly, if a bit warily, John B. replied, "G'day mate. Ah, not that I mind seeing you, but – instinct's going off here – you're here for a reason." It wasn't a question.

The old man's smile disappeared as he nodded.

"Come in," said John B.

Guy walked briskly into the lounge and sat cross-legged on the floor beside Kat. He scratched the cat between the ears.

"Nice place dis," he remarked. "Way way back dere was a meeting place here – de families used to get together every so often, sort problems out, talk about stuff. Dat's where de name Mutumutu came from."

Stewart nodded. "Thanks. Not why you're here though, right?"

"Dere's something crook going on in Alice Springs, mate," the old man replied. "An' more important, somewhere else out dere."

This brought another nod from the wizard. "Cobbemarmoo?" he asked.

If Guy was surprised that Stewart had heard of the place he didn't show it, simply replying, "Yair. Dere. You better get out dere, I reckon."

"A few problems there, mate. First up, I know the name, but I haven't a clue where it is, far less how to get there. Second, even if I knew, I've no way to get there. The only wheels here are on Wilko's Triumph. The key to which is, I think or at least I hope, in the pocket of my old buddy wherever he is. Which leads me to my final point. I've got four mates who went out into town this morning – with a view to finding where this Cobbemarmoo is, oddly enough. Near as I can tell, they haven't come back. The whole point of looking for the place was to find Jazz's boyfriend – now I reckon I've got to find her first. And Wilko. And Darren, and Scarlet. Then we can all go bush together."

Old Black Guy sighed. "You know where your friends are?"

"Nope. Do you?"

"Sorry mate. But I do know where you really need to be. An' it's out dere. In de desert. Like I tol' you, dere's something crook goin' on. It's important I reckon – real important."

John B. found himself grinding his teeth, a habit he'd never realised he had and indeed normally didn't.

The black man saw his tension, rose from the floor and walked behind

Stewart's chair. He reached down and began to knead the neck and shoulder muscles under the purple t-shirt.

"What are you doing? Hey, that's good. That's really good."

John B. closed his eyes and felt some of the tension drain from him as the bony fingers massaged out knots with surprising power. As the bunched muscles loosened he felt his perspective shifting. Yes, there was clearly something wrong – something very wrong. But stressing and fretting weren't going to help. He needed to do something, but he needed to do it calmly and thoughtfully.

Eyes still shut he said, "Sometime when this is all over I must get you to teach me this."

"Reckon you already know," said the old man with a smile in his voice.

"Do I? News to me."

"Instinct. Ya dunno what you can do till you try."

John B. turned that thought over in his mind for a little while as Old Black Guy's massage made him more relaxed than he'd truly felt in weeks.

Finally he opened his eyes and said, "Question. If what's happening at Cobbemarmoo is that important why are you here, and not there? Why do you want me there and not round here?"

Guy looked down at Stewart, and suddenly seemed much, much older. Wearier, too. The massage stopped.

He replied slowly, "We good at different t'ings, you an' me. My… job is to heal. People mostly – dey bodies, minds maybe." Pointing to the bandage on Stewart's hand he continued, "Dat Doc Jones, she work her way, and she's real good y'know, an' me, I work mine. Heal or fix other t'ings, sometimes. Dis… dis is somethin' different. Somethin' I reckon needs you ta do."

"Me, huh? What's my 'job' then do you reckon?"

The old man stared at John B.'s face. They looked into each other's eyes for a timeless time before the leathery black man answered.

"Bit like mine, only bigger. You gotta trust me on dis, brudder. Your friends mebbe doin' it tough – I dunno for sure, but I got a real bad feelin' dat if we don' do somethin' – an' I guess I mean if you don' do something out dere at dat place – well, den everybody's gonna be in a whole lot more trouble."

There was a long silence. John B. sat in the armchair and gazed appraisingly at the old man.

"It's this – magic, isn't it? Ever since I hit my head that time the world seems to have become a whole lot weirder and more complicated."

A little of Old Black Guy's smile creased his face again as he replied, "It's always bin weird an' complicated I reckon. You just seein' it from a different angle dan you been used to lately."

Kat stirred himself from where he'd been curled up watching them both, padded his way around the old man, and then rubbed himself against John

B.'s shins. He made a small peculiar noise that might almost have been 'uh-huh' then stretched back out on the floor and seemingly went back to sleep.

Stewart leaned forward to wipe some of the white fur from his jeans, and nodded. "Okay, I'll take your word for it. Do me a favour and look for the others. If – when you find them let 'em know where I've gone, and tell 'em how to find me."

"Oh, I reckon dey gonna find you alright."

"Mmm. Which still leaves the question of how am I supposed to get out into the middle of the desert? No wheels, remember?"

Old Black Guy looked thoughtful for a minute or two. "Yeah. Reckon I can do somethin' 'bout dat. Take me a little while," he said.

With that he stood up. He stretched then stamped his bare feet before taking a couple of strides toward the front door.

Stopping and turning he said, "I'll be back soon as I can, brudder. You better get some sleep eh? Reckon you be busy tomorrow."

Kat looked up as if in telepathic farewell.

"You too, big fella," said Guy with a grin.

The Persian flicked his tail, then lay his head back down and set about following the 'sleep' advice.

Stewart locked the door after the old man. He looked in the direction of the bedroom he'd been sharing with Darren, and then shook his head briefly.

Instead he went into the kitchen and poured himself a generous measure of Scotch. Glass in hand he returned to the armchair. The whisky disappeared in two large mouthfuls. The wizard breathed deeply, willing his eyes to close and his mind to rest.

"C'mon, man," he said to himself. "You survived that mad bloody witch and the big demon thing in that cavern under the desert. After that, what's gonna bother you?"

Shifting slightly in the chair he then said, "I shouldn't ask myself things like that."

With difficulty he followed the cat to sleep. If it wasn't dreamless then he remembered nothing.

*

It was the early hours of the morning when Guy's gentle knock rapped the front door again. Given the quietness of the sound, the speed with which John B. woke, got to the door and opened it said much for his state of mind. The Scotch and the meditation had helped, but not a lot.

"Brought ya a present," the old man smiled and jerked a thumb over his shoulder.

Stewart could see, parked in the driveway and illuminated by the street light, an old motorcycle with a timber box sidecar bolted to it.

"You ride, don'cha? You got dat look."

"I hear that a bit. Used to. I've not actually ridden for a while but it'll come back to me."

"De useful stuff does," said Guy, nodding.

The two men walked over to examine the machine. There was barely a trace of chrome work, every surface covered with a worn, dusty but remarkably intact coat of matt khaki paint.

"Ariel W/NG. 350cc. Old army bike, still got its old camouflage coat," observed the wizard.

"Yep. 1940. Toughest bike in de world for rough conditions dey used to reckon."

"So I've heard. This one still looks in pretty good nick. Something you – ah, fixed? Where did you… ?"

Guy interrupted quickly. "Dere's always stuff around if ya know where to look."

John B. nodded. "Right enough," he said, and turned to walk back to the house. "Hang on while I change into some clean clothes. I've been in these all day and all night."

"Heh – I been wearin' dis clobber a whole lot longer'n dat!"

"Yeah. But I'm not you, remember?" he said, stalking into the bedroom.

Soon after he was back in the lounge, talking as he dragged a different purple t-shirt over his head.

"Cobbemarmoo," said Stewart, not exactly savouring the word. "It is where the archaeological team are, isn't it?

Old Black Guy was drawing a rough map on a sheet of note paper that he'd just been given.

"You gotta go to de place where de stones stand up first. You get what ya need dere first. Den after dat you follow de nose, eh?"

"Got it. Thanks. You been there?" asked John B. idly as they walked back outside to the motorcycle.

Guy waved a non-committal hand and said, "Oh, lotsa times over de years."

"So what's there?"

"Memories mostly," replied the old man, watching Kat spring lightly into the sidecar. For his size, the big Persian often surprised people with his agility although Guy seemed unsurprised by anything.

Stewart frowned. Something in the tone of the answer bothered him. "Stuff worth remembering?"

Old Black Guy's seemingly perpetual grin disappeared. He looked seriously at Stewart and said, "Sometimes dere's stuff we got to remember to forget."

"Did Possum remember? And then tell this Bevan character something he shouldn't have? Is that what started all this?"

"Possum remembered a bit of what he remembered his grandfather rememberin'."

"And you?"

Guy shrugged and answered, "I remember everythin'. Sometimes."

John B. nodded. "Especially the stuff you remember to forget." It wasn't a question.

"Yeah. Dat especially. Same as you."

The old man patted the bike affectionately. "Tank's full. Look after her, eh?"

"I will. You look after the others, right?"

"Oh, dey be right. Don't worry."

John B. started the Ariel and was momentarily surprised at how quiet it was. Then he realised he hadn't heard it at all when Guy had pulled up in the driveway.

"You okay to get around without the bike?"

Guy's grin was fixed firmly back in place as he scratched Kat's head and replied, "I can always find a way of gettin' where I ought to be. See ya later, brudders – ya got work to do."

"So have you, remember," said Stewart as he set off.

"Always," answered the old man, looking more ancient than ever as a shadow of concern crossed behind his grin.

.o0o.

The two archaeologists had argued over dinner before retiring to their separate tents. That was unusual, as Drayden more typically sank into sullen silence when irritated with his senior colleague (which was often).

"These damned 'you might consider' questions of yours – they're nothing to do with teaching, are they?" Drayden had snapped. "It's just you showing off something that you know and you reckon I don't. You did the same thing at Uni. I bet you did the same thing as a school teacher, didn't you? Proving you were cleverer than a bunch of ten year olds. That's pathetic!"

  Bevan had responded with a dismissive wave and said, "It's about, understanding the true nature of knowledge."

"Bull! It's all about power."

"Ah, and now you, are learning. Knowledge is power."

  Drayden snorted "Cliché! Another bloody cliché. You're full of 'em."

"A cliché becomes such because, of its repetition. That repetition does not diminish, the intrinsic truth which gave rise to it in the, first place. Repetition may dull awareness but does not, change the facts. The Phoenicians understood this. They codified knowledge, and language so that the, learned men could better rule and control the population as they were in turn educated, in their roles."

"Like I said – it's all about power."

Bevan had nodded. "And so, Mr. Drayden, you are learning."

Hours later Drayden lay on his camp stretcher staring at the canvas above. He'd tried to sleep but failed miserably. It could be said that Roderick Drayden did most things miserably.

In his mind's eye he kept seeing Bevan shoot the head off the taipan. The skill with the gun was disconcerting. He'd regarded the professor as an irritating old duffer who'd outlasted his usefulness on the younger man's career path.

It had always been Drayden's intent to maximize his own credit and reward for the discoveries at Cobbemarmoo. It was increasingly obvious that the old fool didn't grasp the commercial possibilities of their work – books, royalties, and celebrity. That Da Vinci business could be so yesterday.

The question of how to sideline the old man had been vexing for a while. The longer they spent with only each other for company the more Bevan went from being an irritant to being an obstacle. But Roderick had always thought that when the time came he'd be an obstacle that would be easily overcome.

The casual ruthless efficiency with which he'd dispatched the snake though… And with a gun which had never even been revealed before… Clearly the old ratbag could be dangerous. Yeah, well, he wasn't the only one.

Drayden sat up and reached for the rum beside his bed. He took a swig straight from the bottle to fortify his resolve. He listened through the canvas for the familiar sound of the professor's heavy breathing as he slept in the neighbouring tent.

"No time like the present," he said to himself.

Silently he pulled on canvas pants and a shirt, his running shoes, and a jacket to keep out the chill air of the night. Into one deep pocket of the jacket he shoved the rum bottle. Into another pocket he slipped the carefully wrapped head of the taipan.

Smiling his unpleasant smile he crept out of his tent.

Walking slowly and carefully so his shoes wouldn't squeak in the sand, Drayden went to the canvas shelter that served as their living area. As he lifted the keys of the four-wheel-drive truck he noticed that the professor's rucksack still lay on the ground beside where he had earlier been sitting.

He gave a tiny snort of delight when he found the revolver still inside it.

'This makes life easier,' he thought. 'I don't have to carry the old bugger's body to the truck – he can walk!'

Giving the gun a satisfied squeeze he made his way to Bevan's tent. Throwing open the tent flap he crouched in the entrance.

"Wake up, old man!" he barked.

Bevan grunted and jolted awake. "Hnn? Eh? What?"

He blinked uncertainly at the figure at the end of the bed.

Drayden brandished the pistol. "Get up, professor. We're going for a drive."

"What? Drayden what are you, playing at?"

"I'm not playing. Not any more."

The younger man hustled his erstwhile mentor out of the tent, not even allowing him time to pull any other clothes over his striped pyjamas.

"Nobody will be surprised at a bloke your age, all the way out here, getting the wanders at night," observed Drayden with a nasty chuckle.

The gun was kept aimed squarely at the professor as he was ordered into the passenger seat of the truck.

"Sit!" was the next order.

Grumbling, Bevan did as he was told, watching as his protégé dashed around and climbed into the driver's seat.

"You have, some plan then I, take it?"

"Like I said – a drive."

The gun in his right hand never wavered despite Roderick's necessarily awkward one-armed driving. Neither man spoke in the fifteen minutes or so for which they travelled into the desert. The headlights blazed a path through the darkness. There was cloud cover – much too high to promise rain but enough to hide much of the usual starlight.

Drayden stopped the vehicle beside a pile of rocks.

"Just the sort of thing you'd go looking for, prof," he said. "Now get out of the truck and sit down over by that big stone."

Bevan wordlessly complied. Drayden allowed himself another swig of rum, never taking his eyes off the professor. Moving at a rather more leisurely pace than usual, he alighted and moved to lean against the front of the vehicle. He patted the pocket that held the snake's head.

"Sorry sir, but you're about to have an unfortunate encounter with the local wildlife."

"Indeed?"

"Oh yeah. An Oxy.. Oxy… ˆwhatever the name was. Taipan. Inland taipan – the deadlier one. Damn shame. Tragic loss really. I'll be sure to write about how heartbroken I was at your death. Add some pathos to the interviews. Probably even sell me a few more copies of the book."

He raised the rum bottle in a mocking toast before downing a large gulp. "First recorded death from the bite of one of these. See, I was listenin' to you. You'll be history, eh?"

Roderick gave a little giggle at his own joke and continued, though his voice was becoming strange. "I won't say 'to your health' obviously, but I s'pose I ought to thank you for the opportun'ty…"

Drayden's brow creased in puzzlement and irritation as he realised he was slurring his words. He drank another mouthful.

"Opp'tun'ty to make m' name. Make m' fortune…"

He grabbed at the bonnet of the truck as he started to sway.

Sitting quite still, Bevan mildly remarked, "Bad combination, rum and, sleeping tablets."

The gun waved vaguely in his direction as its wielder battled to focus.

"I don' take sleepin' tablets."

"No but, I do."

There was a thud as the gun slipped from Drayden's hand and landed on the bonnet.

"And there are several of them dissolved in, your dark rum," the professor continued.

"How'd you know… that I was gonna…?"

"Actually I didn't. I expected to find you helplessly soporific after, your lunchtime tipple tomorrow. I prepared your cocktail while you, were at your ablutions tonight."

With a gurgle the younger archaeologist collapsed to the ground. Bevan continued to sit and watch him.

"You really had no, chance, dear boy. You see I have, a destiny to fulfill. Your rather limited services as my assistant have frankly long since, ceased to outweigh the irritation of your, personality. You do however have a role to play in, that destiny which has delivered you to me. You have much more value to me as…"

Bevan stopped and peered at the unresponsive form slumped in the darkness outside the headlights' beam. There was no sign of rise and fall around the ribs.

"Blast!" the old man snapped, then gave an arthritic groan as he creakily stood up.

Joints protesting in the cold night air he shuffled over to the truck and looked down at the prostrate figure. Unable to bend he settled for kicking Drayden in the side. The only reaction was his own wince as he hurt his already tender foot.

He picked up his gun, the rum and its screw cap from the bonnet. As he resealed the bottle he looked at it with some asperity.

"I really didn't expect he'd be able to consume, so much. A fatal mix was not, what I'd intended."

The small shiver as he climbed into the driver's seat was surely a reaction to the night air and not a moment of doubt about his destiny.

The senior archaeologist managed a laborious three point turn without running over Drayden although that was by chance, not thoughtful design.

"Mm," he mused as he completed the turn. "I wonder how weakened a state Mr. Hunter is in by now? I may have to visit him this afternoon. Perhaps offer a, medicinal rum to help him overcome Drayden's dreadful oversight, regarding his supplies. Mm – my destiny will provide."

As he accelerated back toward his campsite he gave a cursory glance in the mirror and said casually, "Consider this – a marathon is, a handful of spots to die."

Drayden's breathing was very shallow, but he wasn't as deceased as the darkness and the professor's cursory examination had led the old man to believe. Coincidentally, as the professor posed his casual challenge he actually gave a faint groan, but that was lost in the sound of the engine.

Oblivious, Bevan smiled smugly to himself and said, "Of course, the spots on a die, twenty-one, plus a handful, five, add up to the number of, miles in a marathon. Not that you'll be, running any more of, those."

Left for dead in the starlight Drayden gave another soft groan as he finally slipped into complete unconsciousness.

.o0o.

It had turned into a long and frustrating day for Sergeant Conroy. Councillor Atkinson had been more than usually demanding and difficult, then after finally laying that particular vexation to rest he'd realised he was due to put in an appearance at a Chamber of Commerce meeting.

From there he'd had been called on to attend another meeting with some self-important local identities, then off to 'Represent the Police Force' at a Services Club function.

'Community profile' it was called, so he'd been told. Conroy got stuck with it regularly because he actually had quite highly developed diplomatic skills. He had the skills, but not often the enthusiasm for using them.

"I'm just a simple country copper," he said to himself as he trudged up the path to the station house. "All I want to do is keep the peace round here."

If the truth were to be known, Conroy's regular and reassuring presence at so many public functions did go a long way towards maintaining a relatively quiet and trouble-free community in and around his 'patch'. In his heart of hearts he probably even knew that, but the knowledge did little to overcome his frustration at the 'endless bloody bun-fights' that cluttered his days and evenings.

At least a few of those community events were sometimes brightened by the presence of the lovely Dr. Margaret Jones. No such luck today, though. 'Too late to call her tonight' the policeman mused unhappily as he opened the door.

He stopped suddenly and looked around the station house in bafflement. "What on earth is that noise?" he asked.

Bob Sharp, the constable sitting at the duty desk, pointed towards the door of an adjoining room.

"Bloke that Serge brought in earlier," he explained.

Eyebrows raised, Conroy opened the door and walked into what was the anteroom of the station's holding cells.

The sound was coming from a man the sergeant didn't recognise, who was curled up asleep under a police-issue blanket on a bunk in one of the cells. It was snoring. It had to be – the man was clearly asleep and it was clearly the sound he made while he was asleep.

'But…' Conroy thought to himself, 'I reckon calling that 'snoring' is about as inadequate as calling Uluru a big rock.'

He looked in the adjoining cell and was surprised to see a pretty blonde girl stretched out on the hard cell bed, her blanket balled up into a makeshift pillow. She was sound asleep. Even had a little smile on her face, the sergeant noted.

"Wow – how does she sleep through that? The place is echoing!" he asked himself quietly, before leaving and closing the anteroom door.

"Are they part of the 'gang' Steinmetz was going to look into this afternoon?" he asked his constable.

"Guess so, Sarge," was Bob's reply, accompanied by a shrug. "Serge didn't tell me much before he knocked off to go to the gym. Just said to keep 'em locked up, and ignore any bull they might try to tell me."

Conroy nodded slowly. Constable Sharp was not a man who lived up to his name.

"They don't look like international drug runners," observed the sergeant.

"What do international drug runners look like, Sarge?"

There was no hint of irony in Sharp's voice.

"Fair enough question I suppose, Sharpie. Where's Serge's report?"

"Dunno Sarge. Not sure if he's written one yet." Bob Sharp wasn't a big reader. He wasn't illiterate, but he couldn't spell the word either. He tried to have as little to do with reports as possible.

The senior officer sighed and said, "Righto. I'll get it off him tomorrow. Might as well let them sleep. I've got a bloody meeting with the mayor first thing in the morning, then after that I'll go check out this 'drugs lair' on Mutumutu Street."

Conroy gave the night duty man a friendly, casual salute. They'd known each other for a while.

"It won't exactly be a quiet night, eh? Shouldn't be a busy one though, I hope," said the sergeant.

Bob grinned. "Not many of 'em are Sarge. Not during the week, specially."

As he left the station Conroy shook his head and, smiling, said to himself, "I doubt even you could sleep through that noise, Sharpie."

.oOo.

23 SNAKE, CHARMING …

The morning sun was slowly taking the chill from Roderick Drayden's body. His joints ached, and he had what felt to him like the world's worst hangover, but he was alive and awake.

"Old bloody Bevan didn't figure on that," he growled to himself.

Painfully he tried to roll onto his side and get to his feet, but the effort was beyond him.

'Lie here for a bit. Get some sun. Warm up. Take it slow,' he thought. 'Get up in a while. Reckon I know the way back to the camp. Run back. Old bugger won't be expecting that. Won't know what's hit him by the time I'm done.'

With the discipline of the long-distance athlete, Drayden lay on the sand gradually willing his body to co-operate. Whenever he tired of that he thought of what he would do to Walter Bevan when he found him. That motivated him. Then he would think of the glittering future he would make for himself based on the old man's research. Maybe his own TV show on one of those documentary channels. Yeah, that'd be good. He started to move.

*

The scrawled map had long since blown out of the sidecar. Kat had made no move to snare it, apparently unconcerned.

John B. was no more troubled by the loss. He'd already fixed in his head the route to 'the place where the stones stand up' and figured he was well along his way there.

The Ariel was passing a spot where there must have once been a billabong. Perhaps there was still some water deep below ground, the wizard mused, seeing some clumps of tough brown grass and a couple of dead trees. Suddenly Kat yowled loudly from within the sidecar.

"Uh-oh. I know that voice," said John B. "Don't you dare go in there. You're in the middle of the world's biggest sandbox!"

The motorcycle rolled to a halt. Kat jumped to the ground and found a satisfactory patch of sand in which to relieve himself.

'Not a silly thought, really,' mused Stewart. He shut down the purring 350cc motor and followed the Persian's lead against the thin trunk of a desiccated eucalypt.

A brief but satisfying time later he climbed back onto the bike. It didn't start. Simple as that.

He scratched his head, dismounted, and began a careful check. The Ariel W/NG wasn't a complicated machine, especially by modern standards. John B. was no mechanic but he usually knew enough to get by. He was used to British engineering, having done many 'running repairs' on his old Hillman Hunter (blown up recently in one of several failed attempts on the wizard's life).

Whatever was wrong with the bike however was beyond his forensic abilities. It just wouldn't start.

John B. sat on the sand, scratching at his head. Then he reached over and scratched Kat's head, perhaps in the hope a bright idea might spark in either of their brains.

With a little sigh the wizard said to his feline companion, "Oh well, little mate – I guess I oughta wish for someone to come along."

"Mmreh," was the cat's response before padding away to curl up in the limited shade of a sand dune.

He was still sleeping peacefully a half hour later. John B. had tried a few different experiments on the bike in that time, all with the same amount of success: none.

Whatever the wizard might have expected to happen next, it wasn't the arrival of Roderick Drayden jogging unsteadily over the crest of a dune.

Drayden was no less surprised at the sight that met him as he came over the rise. The first thing he saw was the old motorcycle and sidecar, apparently parked in the middle of nowhere. Then he spotted the purple-shirted figure sitting cross legged on the sand beside the bike. He was already scheming as he made his way down the dune and was further stunned to realise that the figure was his erstwhile workmate John B. Stewart.

'Would that make getting hold of the bike easier?' he wondered briefly. Didn't matter. It'd make it more satisfying though.

John B. looked up but didn't stand as the runner approached him. "Morning Dran – er, Roderick. Fancy meeting you here."

'Actually I wouldn't fancy meeting you anywhere,' was what he thought to himself, knowing the feeling was mutual.

Drayden stood bent over, hands on his knees, sucking in deep breaths. He was still feeling decidedly unwell – his malice-fuelled exertions had helped him focus past the discomfort but the professor's drugged rum was still affecting him.

He pulled himself together and replied, "Stewart. Didn't expect – pant – to find you – pant – out here. Didn't know you – pant – had a bike."

"Probably a lot you don't know about me, mate," observed the wizard with casual understatement before remarking, "You don't look too flash. Overdone the run this morning?"

If it had occurred to him that it was unusual for even the most eccentric of joggers to run in canvas pants and a button down shirt, he gave no indication of it.

The archaeologist stretched and stood upright with some effort. "I've felt better," he admitted. "Bit of a reaction to something, I think." He indicated the sidecar. "Any chance of a lift?"

Stewart surprised himself by saying honestly, "I would if I could mate. Unfortunately the old Ariel's broken down on me."

"Your radio doesn't work? So what?"

"No – Ariel. The bike. That's what make it is. Old British job, saw service in the War."

Drayden looked disparagingly at the machine. "Which one? Crimea?"

With a dry smile John B. got up and walked back to the machine replying, "Not quite that far before your time. I'll keep trying to fix it."

Kat woke but didn't get up. Instead he raised his head to watch from a safe distance.

John B. knelt beside the bike, concentrating on trying to trace the broken wire he was sure was the problem. Behind him Drayden quietly took a thickly wrapped cling-film package from the pocket of the jacket tied around his waist. Silently he rolled some of the clear plastic back upon itself, revealing the head of the dead Oxyuranus microlepidotus.

The archaeologist squeezed the sides of the taipan's head to force open the jaws. With a lunge he clamped the jaws onto Stewart's arm, shifted his grip and squeezed hard to pump the deadly contents of the venom glands down the fangs.

The wizard gasped, pitched and rolled himself away. He stood quickly but unsteadily, and looked down at the grisly object still attached to his arm.

"Drano you lousy…" Stewart began, and reeled towards Drayden.

The archaeologist skipped backwards, and continued to nimbly dodge away until John B. staggered a final time and fell to the sand.

Stewart looked up and as his eyes glazed managed to mumble "I wish… you won't… get… away…"

He lost consciousness before the words "with this" could be uttered.

"Right then," said Drayden to himself, rubbing his hands together. He walked over to the bike, climbed on, and had exactly the same amount of success trying to start it that Stewart had had. "Damn it! He wasn't bloody lying to me! It is stuffed!"

It says a lot about Roderick Drayden's character that he'd automatically assumed that Stewart had lied and simply hadn't wanted to help. That was what he would have done.

Drayden slapped a frustrated hand on the fuel tank of the bike. Cursing under his breath he climbed back off the old Ariel, kicked the front tyre, and started to jog away.

He'd barely gone a half dozen paces when he stopped in his tracks, hearing a strange and unexpected sound. It was… what? Surely not… hoof beats?

Suddenly the source of the hoof beats was revealed. A camel appeared over a nearby dune at a gallop. On its back, riding in a rickety home-made saddle, was Old Black Guy.

The old man saw John B. sprawled on the sand and brought the camel to an immediate stop. The animal knelt and the rider clambered off to check on the prone figure.

With an evil grin Drayden sprinted towards the camel, with the clear intent of leaping into the saddle and riding away with all possible speed. Suddenly Kat uncurled and ran at the camel from the opposite direction. The white Persian jumped and hissed at the much bigger animal just as Drayden got to it shouting, "This will do me, you old black bast…"

The startled camel reared up to its two-metre height at speed. On the way a hard skull with four hundred kilos of dromedary behind it caught Drayden squarely on the point of the chin. The archaeologist's jaw was slammed shut with a snap.

A little spray of blood spattered across the sand as a large forward portion of Drayden's tongue spun through the air. Drayden himself flew briefly in the opposite direction before he landed half-stunned. In shock he watched Kat pounce on the severed flesh, seize it in his own jaws and bolt away around a dune.

Old Black Guy looked up from the unconscious John B. and glared angrily at the would-be camel thief. "You sit dere an' don' move till I be ready to work on you!" the old man barked.

Drayden sprawled, transfixed by Guy's baleful glare, only dimly aware of the blood streaming from his mouth.

The old man went back to his examination of the wizard. He muttered as much to himself as Stewart. "Funny sort o' bite. Never seen anyone bit by a dead snake. Least ways, not one been dead so long. Ah don' know dat de poison gonna work so good no more, eh?"

He quickly built a small fire of dry grass and pieces of a convenient long-dead tree, and then pulled a variety of leaves, stems and seeds from different pockets of his vest and trousers. First he worked them together with a good spit of saliva in the palm of his hand, and then he smeared the resulting paste onto the end of a long branch that he proceeded to warm over the fire.

Muttering to himself, he then spread the paste onto the wound on John B.'s arm. He patted the poultice gently and said, "Right den – give dat some time."

With a sigh of evident reluctance the old man walked over to where Drayden sat staring but not moving, blood still running from the corners of his mouth.

"Hmph. Reckon you in shock mebbe, fella," he said as he tilted the archaeologist's head forward to drain some blood, then back. "Open yer mouth."

Drayden complied, his jaw opening slackly. Old Black Guy jammed a hot piece of wood straight from the fire into the blood-soaked mouth. "Bite on dis! You bite hard!" he commanded.

Briefly, clumsily, Drayden tried to struggle to his feet. Failing utterly, he slumped back to the ground and groaned as he bit down on the cauterizing wood. As the searing stick did its work his eyes rolled back in his head and he passed out.

Kat padded back and sat quietly at the old man's feet.

"Nasty t'ing you was carryin' dere big fella. Sorta t'ing dat's caused a lot o' trouble along de way, I reckon. Got rid of it, did ya?"

The Persian licked some sand from his paw, possibly getting a sour taste out of his mouth.

Old Black Guy checked on the cat's housemate, who was already starting to stir back to consciousness. The black man gently wiped his patient's forehead and lifted a sweaty lock of hair from over one eye.

"Thanks," mumbled the wizard.

Guy smiled, nodded, and patted the shoulder of the purple shirt. He turned to check on his other patient, less solicitous of comfort but assuring himself that he was breathing. "You wasn't quite right before ya got dat whack, was ya?" he said. "Mebbe not a good combination I'm t'inkin'. Mebbe you be not quite right when ya wake up, either."

Flexing his hands the old healer turned his attentions to the Ariel.

His long fingers were still delicately probing the bike's inner workings when John B. was able to open his eyes and keep them open. Instinctively the wizard went to scratch at the poultice on his arm.

"Better not touch dat jus' yet," advised Guy without looking up.

Stewart nodded, and smiled as Kat licked his hand. With the comfort of old friends they sat together, and as John B.'s head gradually cleared they watched the aboriginal elder at work.

The old man had chewed briefly on a twig to produce a makeshift brush.

This he repeatedly inserted deep into the Ariel's engine from different angles, regularly wiping anything stuck to the twig's end onto his ancient trousers.

Eventually he gave a satisfied chuckle, stood and with a flourish started the bike. Kat purred and John B. applauded as he got to his feet.

Guy patted the fuel tank of the previously recalcitrant Ariel, now humming like a contented sewing machine.

"Sorry 'bout de bike," he said. "She'll be right now."

John B. looked at the motorcycle, just a little dubiously. "Okay. She only stops when she has to, eh?"

"Right," agreed Old Black Guy.

Stewart flexed his bandaged hand. "This is feeling a lot better, too."

"Tol' you dat Doc Jones was good, eh?"

"You also said you'd try to find Darren and the others. Any news?"

"I tol' you – dey'll be okay."

Clearly Stewart was going to get no further information on that front. 'I'm not to be distracted?' he wondered.

"Dat fella you're lookin' for, you're on de right track."

"Glad to hear it. Any clues on what to do after I find him?"

The old man smiled and replied, "Follow de nose, mate!" As he spoke he tapped the side of his own weather-beaten nose.

"Fair enough," replied the wizard. "You right with… that?" He jerked a thumb over his shoulder at the unconscious wreckage of Roderick Drayden.

"Yeah. I'll toss 'im on de back o' de camel, take him to town. Somebody'll look after 'im if he's lucky."

Stewart rolled his eyes. "Be more luck than he deserves," he said without remorse.

Old Black Guy tilted his head sideways, then winked and said, " Reckon he's got what he deserves. Look at 'im. He won't do nobody no harm."

John B. nodded. "Fair call," he said.

"Don' pick at dat," cautioned the healer, indicating the poultice on Stewart's arm. "It'll fall off when it's dried up an' ready. You better get goin' I reckon."

Before getting back on the bike John B. clasped the old man's hand. "Thanks mate," he said with deep sincerity.

"We do what we gotta do, brudder."

With a smile and a nod the wizard gave the engine a few experimental revs. "Come on, Kat," he called.

The big Persian rubbed a smear of white fur onto the brittle fabric of Old Black Guy's trouser leg, pressing hard against the bony shin.

"So long, big fella. You keep lookin' after him, eh?"

A flick of the long tail, and the cat jumped into the sidecar. John B. gave a determined thumbs up then gunned the Ariel away.

Guy walked over to Drayden, who still lay unconscious. He grabbed the archaeologist's shirt and with a strength that belied the obvious age of his wiry frame the healer hoisted his patient up and onto the back of the placidly kneeling camel. Then he climbed into his rickety saddle.

"Not up to us no more, mate," he said giving the long neck of the camel an affectionate pat as the animal stood up. The beast started to plod in the direction of Alice Springs. Old Black Guy made no effort to hurry it.

.o0o.

Sound travels a long way in the desert. So Walter Bevan heard the sound of an approaching vehicle long before he could see it.

His first reaction was irritation, but then that was Bevan's first reaction to just about everything. A moment's reflection seemed to change his mood. He was puzzled, yes, but quite calm as he carefully closed and stacked all the notebooks he'd had laid out on the camp table.

He was calm enough to prepare himself a cup of tea, which he was sipping as the source of the engine noise arrived at the edge of the campsite, stopping in a cloud of red dust.

The vehicle was a stylish (and clearly expensive) BMW four-wheel-drive. Its normally pristine white paintwork wore an overcoat of desert sand. The door opened and out stepped Carl Costelow.

With some effort the lawyer adopted a polite smile as he entered the canvas shelter.

"Professor Bevan. Good to see you again," he lied smoothly.

"Mr. Costelow. You are an unexpected, visitor to be sure but, not unwelcome," the archaeologist replied, with a sincerity his visitor neither recognised nor would have understood.

The professor shook the hand offered in habit before continuing, "You have some purpose in, calling on, us. A long journey for a, social call."

Costelow was not by nature a patient man, and the drive had frayed his temper, but he made an effort to control himself and be civil. He'd spent the journey dreaming up scenarios about what he might find, and until he got a real clue he may have to keep on the right side of the old man.

The problem was that Bevan didn't really have a right side. Even if he did, Carl was too abrasive by nature to stay on it.

With thin politeness Costelow began by observing, "I was lucky to find you, actually. I thought you were supposed to be working somewhere northwest of here? That's what you said when you came to me 'investigating the legalities' of this excavation you wanted to do."

Bevan nodded slowly without answering. He was musing to himself – 'Ah well, I knew I couldn't hope to keep my activities a total secret. I had hoped to direct any unwanted attentions away from here.'

The lawyer's fragile temper began to unravel further. "Well?" he snapped. "If it wasn't for a chance encounter with that scrawny bad-tempered off-sider of yours I'd have never known where you were."

"Ah – Mr. Drayden. Of course," replied the professor. To himself he thought, 'It seems I was right to dispense with his services.' To Costelow he said, slightly apologetically, "Archaeology is sometimes a, rather inexact discipline I'm afraid. The location in which I expected to, be concentrating my labours turned out to be, less fruitful than what I have in this place. Anyway here I am and here, you are. What can, I do for you?"

"Explain to me why you're here!"

Bevan shrugged. "Conducting an archaeological survey on behalf, of a number of Universities. You know that. We discussed it in your, office."

"Why here? Your mate dropped a clue that you were onto something special. Well, if there's any treasure to be found out here it rightfully belongs to my people!"

"Pardon? Your people?" asked the professor, looking quizzically at the man standing opposite him. His hair was curly, certainly, but he looked paler in skin colour than the weather-beaten Drayden.

"Damn right!" was the belligerent reply. "The traditional owners of the land, we're called you know. And I'm their legal representative."

"We, or they? Perhaps you could make up your mind. But there is I'm afraid no, 'treasure' as you put it. I am here for, purely scientific reasons."

Costelow sneered. "I don't believe you. 'Sitting on something' the skinny bloke said. I want to know what, and I want my share. On behalf of my people."

"Oh dear," sighed Bevan. "Who else have you talked to about this?"

"Nobody yet." Carl thought to himself, 'I'm not fool enough to be sharing whatever it is you've found here'.

After another sigh Bevan said, "We might consider, this conversation to be like a broken pencil…"

"It is not pointless! I demand that you share the treasures of this land!"

The archaeologist shook his head as he stood and gestured to the excavation. "I assure you Mr. Costelow there is, no such thing. Clearly though my word is not sufficient, for you. I invite you to investigate the operation here – see for yourself, look around."

For several minutes the lawyer did exactly that. He paced around the campsite.

He contorted himself awkwardly, looking under the overhang. Without a torch the artwork couldn't be seen, and there was nothing else in the narrow space to catch Costelow's interest.

He returned to the campsite proper, forced politeness making him try to be surreptitious about peering into boxes and tents. When that turned up no evidence of 'treasure' he went back out into the sun. He tried vainly to disguise his increasing frustration at being unable to locate the valuable hoard he'd convinced himself must be there somewhere. He was reduced to even running his fingers through some of the heaps of sifted dirt.

Bevan stood calmly under the shade of the canvas shelter, watching his agitated visitor. He kept an eye on his notebooks, but knowledge was not the valuable commodity that was being looked for by the rapacious lawyer.

Eventually Costelow returned to the shelter, flushed and sweating.

"It is unpleasant out there isn't it? I do find the conditions at this, time of day too hot for, much outdoor work," said the archaeologist. "Can I offer you a drink?" he continued solicitously. "I'm sure that Mr. Drayden wouldn't object, to your having some of his rum."

After the air-conditioned comfort of the BMW Costelow found he was wheezing in the desert heat and could only manage a nod of his head.

"I'm sorry your journey seems, to have been in vain," the professor said as he poured a generous amount of the dark liquid into a tin cup. "No crystal skulls or legendary goblets here I'm, afraid."

Carl had just enough politeness to accept the much-needed drink without snapping at the mild bait.

"Thanks," he managed before downing most of the cup's contents in a single gulp.

"That didn't touch the, sides did it? It is especially hot today. Another?"

The lawyer nodded and held out the cup. It was refilled and drained again quickly.

Costelow looked down at the empty cup. His surly frown deepened as he asked, "Where is the miserable sod, anyway? Not that I mind drinkin' 'is booze."

"Mr. Drayden has shown what I have always, thought an inexplicable fondness for, long distance running." It wasn't a lie. The technical term would be 'obfuscation' – a tactic that the lawyer would have approved of in his professional capacity.

Costelow swayed as he replied, "Runnin'? Out in that heat? Bloody mad! I've lived out here for years an' even I'm strugglin'…" He slipped off the canvas stool he'd parked himself on. "Wha' the…? Heat don' usually get to me this much. Feel like… like…"

Whatever it was that Carl Costelow felt like was lost as he toppled face first into the sand.

With his boot the professor levered the lawyer onto his side, and gave a satisfied nod when he saw that his victim was still breathing.

"Destiny provides. Consider this my, acquisitive friend - Proust refined insensibility," Bevan remarked to the lawyer who was, indeed, in a stupor.

Then the professor proceeded to drag Costelow to a spot a little away from the campsite with the enthusiasm and energy of a man half his his age. His destiny continued to manifest itself – he knew that with a certainty he'd felt ever since Mikkel Krieg's casual conversation had first pointed him in this direction. Authority, the real authority that came with real power, would soon be his. There was something like a spring in his step as he started to assemble a range of carefully prepared items around the unconscious figure.

He even chuckled as he said, "Thank you in advance for, your contribution. It is indeed a far far better thing you, do than you have ever, done before."

.o0o.

John B. had a better grasp of the topography around him than some acquaintances might have expected, and had done a good job of committing Old Black Guy's rough map to memory. As he guided the Ariel across the sands he was confident he was putting the pieces together well.

So he was more satisfied than relieved when he rounded a large dune and got his first sight of Professor Bevan's 'second site'.

He was relieved though, that as he approached he could make out a lean, dark-haired figure sitting tranquilly in the lotus position under a canvas awning.

Stewart stopped the bike beside the shelter, dismounted and approached the meditative man who looked up and smiled.

The wizard returned the smile and said, "Doctor Hunter, I presume?"

Harlan extended a hand. "You presume correctly, sir. Who do I have the honour of addressing?"

The proffered hand was clasped warmly. "John B. Stewart. I'm a friend of a young lady who has been very bloody worried about you."

The archaeologist's smile clouded. "Jazz? Is she alright? I was annoyed at myself that I hadn't contacted her earlier, and then had no way to do so. There was nothing I could do about it but I didn't want to think of her being upset."

"No, not pleasant. I've had a glimpse of her being upset at someone. But if you're okay I reckon she'll be better."

Harlan stood, a little unsteadily, bracing himself on Stewart's shoulder. "Okay. Yes, well, I could be better, but I certainly could be worse. I probably would have been soon if you hadn't come along. So 'okay' is a fair description, I think. You haven't any food in your vehicle have you? I must admit to being a bit hungry."

"Sorry mate, all that's in the sidecar is…"

John B.'s voice trailed off as Kat jumped out of the sidecar, clutching in his jaws a paper bag which turned out to contain a slightly dry ham sandwich. Simple fare, but the Hawaiian couldn't hide his pleasure as he ate it in slow careful mouthfuls.

The wizard patted Kat as he watched the man eat. "That Guy thinks of everything, eh? You did very well not munching into that yourself, little mate."

The Persian purred at the compliment.

"Food shortage?" mused Stewart. "I notice there's a shortage of any other members of your team."

Harlan explained what had happened from the time he'd been collected from the airport by Bevan and Drayden, including the discovery of the empty provision boxes.

John B. nodded and said, "I had a feeling something was dodgy about Walter Bevan but I couldn't figure what. Nothing Rod Drayden did would surprise me any more. Still, I reckon the bastard won't be causing anyone else grief like that again." Seeing Harlan's quizzical look he continued, "Let's just say he got what he deserved."

Hunter nodded, "Things have a way of balancing out, I believe."

"Mmm. The old bloke that pointed me at you was very worried about something happening out here – something that needs stopping. He said I'd find what I needed here. You, presumably. Any ideas?"

"Er… well… not as such. Nothing clear." The archaeologist looked bemused.

"Okay, nothing clear. Let's look at the obscure. What was a specialist in Mediterranean history like Bevan doing in the middle of the Australian desert?"

The two men sat down as Harlan explained about the carvings found at the two sites.

"Intriguing really. Pacific prehistory is more my specialty, but this seems irrefutable evidence of contact with ancient Mediterranean people. We know that there was a complex trading system operating in this country thousands of years ago. There were various tribes travelling north to barter with visitors from parts of Asia. Further to that, then, it's not inconceivable that some merchants could have made it to the Pacific from Europe – it's been theorized before. So those Mediterranean traders connect with what we'd now call Indonesians or Moluccans, for instance, who in turn pass their new goods, knowledge and experiences to their trading partners in Australia. To be honest, I was expecting something in support of that hypothesis to be what Bevan had found."

"It's not, though, is it?" asked the wizard.

"Er, no. Do you have some insights?"

Stewart shook his head. "Not yet. But I reckon there must be more to this than a list of who traded what and with whom. I can't see a place where trading records were scratched into the rock becoming any sort of sacred site. Or a taboo one, if I read Guy's concerns right. I mean, accounts and ledgers can be deadly dull, but not often dangerous as such."

"I've certainly never liked them," conceded the archaeologist with a smile. "But no, these carvings seem to be more… religious in nature. Religion or ritual, perhaps, if I can distinguish between the two. My guess, perhaps I should say concern given his behavior, is that Professor Bevan had some particular ideas about them."

"I'm curious about Bevan," said John B. "The little bit of biography I read about him seemed, well, unspectacular. But clearly he's got something more than a mean streak, abandoning you out here to starve or die of thirst. Unless it was that bloody Drayden acting without the old bloke's knowledge. He's vicious enough, but I wouldn't have thought he had that much initiative."

"Mr. Drayden did come across as bitter."

"He was twisted before he was bitter," observed Stewart wryly.

The Hawaiian grinned. "I'll take your word for that. But as much as it pains me to cast aspersions on a fellow academic, I rather think that nothing happens on this project without Professor Bevan's very direct guidance."

"Which brings me back to the what and the why. Like I said, what I read about Bevan painted a pretty unremarkable picture. And nothing that gave a clue to anything that would have brought him way out here."

"He mentioned hearing some initial hints from a European colleague who I wasn't familiar with, then learning more from a local indigenous fellow in a bar."

Stewart nodded. "That'd be Possum. We've met. Whatever he said, he's been kicking himself for it ever since. It seems to have taken the old Prof out of his usual field of expertise and into… something different. Something he's apparently willing to kill you for, or because of. Just what though?"

Hunter indicated one of the sketches of the Site 1 carvings that he'd drawn from memory.

"This symbol represents Yam-nahar, one of the three major gods of the people we now call Phoenician. God of the sea."

"A nation of sailors. Makes sense a sea-god would be important to them."

"Yes, but not really a nation. Well, there wasn't really a Phoenicia. That's

a name that's come to be applied to a number of sea-faring city states –
Tyre, Sidon, Serepta to name a few - that were prominent a thousand or so
years B.C."

 John B. tapped at one of the upright stones. "Same age as the work done
to make these something more than your average rock?" he asked.

 The Hawaiian shrugged and replied, "Impossible to tell really. I haven't
found anything here we could carbon-date. The style of the artwork fits,
or it could be older. It doesn't look local."

"I didn't think there was a lot of rock carving in this country. More rock
painting."

"Certainly there is more painting known, some of it very old. Carving's
not common, but it's around. What makes these interesting is the style –
I'm not aware of anything like them anywhere in the Pacific. That alone
would have been enough to get Professor Bevan's attention. These look
like a primitive form of something that we'd expect to find somewhere in
the south of the Mediterranean."

"So do you think there were Phoenicians or whatever here, or are these
local work?"

"Someone who was familiar enough with them to copy the style?
Possible – we know they were great seafarers and traders. I suppose there
may have been some intermarriage even. The preservation of something
from 'home', or perhaps just the copying of something they've seen and
been impressed by," pondered the archaeologist.
190

"I wonder who the Phoenicians got their ideas from?" mused John B. In a corner of his mind's eye was a dream of a small boat on a fire-lit sea.

Harlan looked at him with a raised eyebrow and said, "You do think outside the square, don't you?"

"Easy when you don't know where the lines are drawn," he replied. Stewart looked around at the expanse of sand. "Funny place for a sea god."

Harlan waved his notepad vaguely and said, "Looking at this, well, it's a bit disturbing."

"How so? I thought they looked pretty good for something done on memory."

"Um, thank you, but I meant the content. The transcribed artwork itself is as accurate as I can make it. It talks about reawakening the power of Yam-nahar, about Yam-nahar's 'destiny to rule over all'. In particular it seems to mention mastery of the elements. And about the need for a human sacrifice. Quite an unusual one, I think."

John B. was quiet for a few moments. "And which 'bit' of this do you find disturbing?"

"Well… all of it really."

"Good. So we're agreed on that. You think that Bevan may actually be able to pull off this 'reawakening' of godly power?"

"It's very ancient," said Harlan, scratching at his beard. "It goes back over a thousand years before any real reliable records we have of this religion. And those records that we do possess had been heavily influenced by the Greeks and Romans – this is the original stuff."

"The stuff of legends."

"Oh yes. I mean, there are Biblical references to the gods of the Canaanites. Another name used for the Phoenicians. False gods they're described as of course. Baal is one that gets a mention that some people remember, but clearly as a pantheon they're recognized and their worship is at least given some credence."

"Sea gods – let me think. The Prince of Tyre. 'You have said 'I am a god, I sit in the seat of the gods in the heart of the seas.' Ezekiel, Chapter 28."

Hunter showed none of the surprise that Scarlet, Wilko or even Darren would have expressed at Stewart's knowledge of Biblical scripture. Harlan was the sort of academic who was so familiar with his own encyclopaedic mind, and so engrossed in his own field, that he rather vaguely assumed that everyone else's brains worked the same way.

"Yes," he said. "You should always be prepared to consider the truth which is the core of any legend."

John B. took the proffered notepad and flicked through the pages of Harlan's sketches. "I take it this is the sacrifice?" he asked, indicating one particular panel.

It showed an altar table with a notch in the centre, apparently representing a hole, under which was a large bowl. Beside the table stood a robed bearded figure with arms raised. Two lines of characters were depicted above and below the picture.

"That's right," said Harlan. "The inscription – text – is incredibly ancient so my translation is very rough, I'm afraid. 'Here drain the body' … 'our greatest? Most powerful maybe, magic, for the greatest of the gods is with us and his power is with us'. It might be 'in' not 'with', and I'm not at all sure about the word magic."

"A lot of people aren't," observed Stewart. "So this wizard in the robe…"

"Possibly a priest."

"He might have called himself that, but in my book if you're working magic, by whatever name you call it, you're a wizard. He's about to drain the blood from someone or something to make the magic happen?"

Hunter nodded, still with a look of deep concern. "Close. Pretty definite it's someone, not something, by the particular word for 'body'. But I'm not sure about blood – this symbol looks like 'water', maybe 'the water of life' – I suppose that could be interpreted as blood," he said uncertainly.

Stewart actually grinned as he answered, "Water of life – the old Gaelic term that gave us the word 'whisky'. I wonder if a bottle of single malt would do instead?"

He turned his attention back to Harlan's sketch, and his smile disappeared as suddenly as it had come. He looked troubled as he asked, "So if this stuff you remember from Bevan's site is the story of Yam-thingummy and how to bring him to life…"

"Yam-nahar. According to the fragments we've got the story says that he was never killed, as other gods of his, um, stature were. He's described as being laid to rest, and looking at one of these carvings in particular I think that can be taken to mean quite clearly 'not dead, just sleeping'. Sorry to interrupt."

"No worries. But like I was saying, if the carvings you've drawn based on what you saw at the other spot are about waking the god, then what's the story with all this here?" the wizard asked, indicating the surrounding stones.

"Hard to tell," admitted the archaeologist. "Remember, we really don't have anything this old to compare it to. The scattering of old Phoenician or Canaanite records that we've got are mostly pretty dull stuff like the trade records you were alluding to before."

There was a silence as Harlan thoughtfully walked the length of the exposed flat stone carvings then re-examined the bases of the standing stones.

"The two sites are similar. A variation on a theme, perhaps. This one's more of… a warning?"

John B. nodded. "One tells how to do it. This one tells why not to do it."

Harlan cocked his head on his shoulder. "I think you're right," he said. "Where did you get that from?"

"Dunno. When you said 'a warning' it just sort of came to me."

Hunter stared long and hard at the tall stone John B. sat in the shade of. Quietly he said, "I think we need to find Professor Bevan. He may not know the damage he might do."

"Worse still, I think he does. Come on Kat. You too, Harlan."

The archaeologist gathered up his notebooks and small satchel of belongings. He looked worried as he said, "I'll have to tell my University something. Bevan's too, I suppose."

"Well, let's see. The old bloke's off his nut and wants to kill someone, possibly with a view to taking over the world. His off-sider was last seen a gibbering wreck out in the middle of nowhere. It seems likely the two of them tried to kill you and make it look like an accident. So, in short and to sum up: the project's not going well. You could try telling them that, assuming of course that the Prof doesn't succeed in whatever he's trying to do. And thus you'll be in any position to be writing to someone. If he does succeed then we have to wonder whoever or whatever will be left to write to."

"You think it may be that serious?"

"Reanimating a god? Serious? Your guess is as good as mine." The wizard's thoughts briefly turned back to the demon Shub-Niggurath he'd had a brief but memorable confrontation with. "Let's just say I'm prepared to take the idea of 'a warning' seriously. Especially one that's stuck in the local racial memory for so long."

Stewart paused while Hunter pondered this, then asked, "Can you find our way back to this 'Site 1'?"

"Sorry. I've got a photographic memory for some things but I'm afraid directions aren't on that list. Somewhere… that way I think?" offered the archaeologist, pointing vaguely to his right.

John B. looked doubtful. "Old Black Guy said to 'follow the nose'. I don't think he meant mine."

He gestured towards Kat. The big Persian was standing staring into the distance, his tail waving in a wide arc. His pink nose, lightly crusted with sand, was pointing in a direction about a hundred degrees left of where Harlan had suggested.

The archaeologist shrugged and said, "That could work, too."

John B. grabbed the handlebar of the Ariel and nodded toward the sidecar.

"Harlan, would you mind letting our navigator sit on your lap?"

"I'd be honoured," Hunter replied as he climbed into the capsule. "Young sir?" he said, addressing Kat.

With a small "*Mmreh*" the Persian padded over and jumped in.

"I wish we get this right," said Stewart quietly to himself as he stepped onto the motorcycle and gunned it into life.

.oOo.

196

26 THAT SUCKS

The rum and sleeping tablet cocktail had done its work well.

While Costelow remained oblivious, Bevan carefully paced out a large flat area of ground. He meticulously removed any stray windblown camp litter and trod down any sizeable irregularities in the sandy surface.

Satisfied, he then carried out to the middle of the clearing what appeared at first glance to be an ordinary low-slung canvas stretcher bed – the sort of uncomfortable single sleeping option endured by stubborn or hardy campers for years. But symbols had been drawn on either end of the bed frame – symbols that could also be found carved into the Cobbemarmoo sandstone and transcribed into the Professor's notebook.

And in the middle of the canvas bed a hole had been cut. It was about the diameter of one of the tin mugs that Bevan and Drayden had routinely used.

Directly under the hole Bevan placed a large white ceramic mixing bowl. This too had several symbols drawn on it in heavy black marking pen by the Professor's steady hand.

Bevan chatted to the unconscious Costelow as he tied the lawyer firmly to the modified camp stretcher. He wouldn't have considered it a sign of nervousness – he expressed too much confidence in his destiny to allow any suggestion of uncertainty, even to himself. It was more a matter of showing off to a captive audience. If that audience couldn't actually hear him – well, he wouldn't be argued with, would he?

"I had entertained the, notion that young Drayden might have, been my sacrifice of choice. His perfidy in attempting, to eliminate me for some fancied academic glory or commercial gain, or perhaps it was perverse, revenge for some imagined slight – well, I confess it distracted, me. Clouded my judgement. But lo and, behold now your misguided search for treasure, mere, worldly wealth has delivered you, to me. Once again my destiny is, made manifest."

The professor strode back to his tent, and after a few moments rummaging produced from his case a carefully wrapped package. With great solemnity he removed the paper and lifted the black fabric within.

He flicked his wrists in a way that would have done a stage conjuror proud. The material unfolded and was revealed to be Walter Bevan's treasured academic gown. The professor's chest swelled with remembered pride as he donned the robe. It symbolized accomplishment beyond the dreams of generations of struggling farmers. How fitting, then, that it should serve as his robe as he accomplished something undreamed of for millennia. Unconsciously he rubbed a delicate thumb and forefinger along the satin edge as he walked back to the clearing.

He picked up one of his notebooks – a very particular one, and opened it to a very particular page. His brow creased in concentration, his lips moved soundlessly as he again impressed the strange syllables into his memory. With a final nod he placed the book on the ground.

198

Two purposeful strides later Bevan stood beside the bound figure of the activist lawyer.

Carl Costelow's senses began to clear slightly, just in time for him to open his eyes and blearily see a figure robed in black standing over him with arms raised.

"Ur…?" was all he managed to croak out.

"Wrong civilization," remarked Bevan mildly before commencing the incantation he'd taught himself.

To Costelow's ears they didn't sound like words. Just a strange sequence of sounds. There was no way of knowing whether the Professor's characteristic fractured mode of speech was in evidence among the unfamiliar syllables.

But even through his dulled senses Costelow was aware of an uncomfortable feeling of pressure building in the air above him. In the space between the professor's raised hands and the lawyer's body the air seemed to shimmer.

Carl's last sight was of what looked like a small glowing disc forming from nothing directly above him. Abruptly the disc plunged down through the lawyer's stomach, through the hole in the camp stretcher and into the bowl.

The sound was like a gumboot being pulled from thick wet mud. Costelow didn't hear it. He was already dead.

After carefully counting off forty-nine seconds, Walter Bevan reached under the camp bed, and drew out the bowl. It was half full of a bright silver liquid. The surface looked like a polished mirror, but strangely it didn't reflect the professor's face as he gazed into it.

"Well that was, easy," he said.

Without a backward glance he walked back to the shelter and very carefully placed the bowl on the table. Then he removed his gown, folded it neatly and laid it beside the bowl.

The professor strode back out into the sun, and pausing only briefly to wipe sweat from his forehead before starting to prepare another large clearing. This one was on the opposite side of the tent from the camp stretcher on which lay a dry brown husk that was all that remained of Carl Costelow.

.oOo.

Constable Sharp had long since finished his shift and gone home, keen to catch up on some sleep having been prevented from enjoying his usual light snooze by the echoing noise of snoring. So whilst Sharpie was basically a decent man he was less perturbed than he might normally have been when Serge Steinmetz arrived at the station early announcing that he was 'gonna have some fun with the prisoners'.

The burly blonde policeman had started out by waking them, as roughly as possible, by clanging a metal rod against the bars of Wilko's cell.

The Tasmanian woke with a start and roused immediately. In truth, so did Jazz, but just to annoy the policeman she made more of a pretence of waking leisurely. She stretched, looked around and smiled.

"Ah, the butler's arrived. I'll have two muffins, a fried egg, and two strips of bacon please," she said.

"Ha bloody ha. What makes you think you're gonna get any breakfast from me?" sneered Steinmetz.

Jazz's false smile didn't slip as she replied, "You're clearly not a real policeman, so I figured you might be the hired help."

"What do you mean, I'm not a real policeman?"

Wilko groaned softly. "She's not helping," he muttered under his breath.

If the blonde girl heard him she gave no sign of it. "Even if he wasn't smart enough to ask us any intelligent questions, a real copper should have known enough to have at least told us why we're being held here."

"Oh, you want questioning, eh? Alright, Blondie, where's the rest of your gang? I went round your place again this morning on my way here and there's nobody home. Pretty suspicious I reckon."

Wilko and Jazz exchanged worried looks.

"It certainly does sound suspicious," the English girl conceded.

"Um… gang?" asked Wilko.

Steinmetz gripped the bars of the smaller man's cell and leaned towards him. "Yeah, gang. The rest of the drug runners we got told about."

"Drug runners?" repeated the Tasmanian, his blank look accurately reflecting the extent to which he had any idea of what the policeman was talking about.

"You heard me. I know all about what you were up to in the Tavern the other night."

Jazz tried to look around the broad frame of the body builder as she said to Wilko, "This sounds like it's got the fingerprints of that nasty ex-mate of yours on it. Of course, it'd take a real policeman to realize that. You know that this lummox wouldn't spot them."

The big man spun to face her in her cell. "Lummox? You're really starting to annoy me, y'know." He rubbed his hand on his holster in an unconscious gesture that was perhaps affectionate but certainly

202

threatening. "Okay," he continued, "You want questioning, I'll give you questioning."

Grabbing the keys from a hook, Serge unlocked the cells and at gunpoint ushered the pair into the office.

"You sit in that chair there, Blondie, and watch while I have some fun with your boyfriend. Extracting information, I call it."

Steinmetz lifted the front of his shirt and rippled his abdomen muscles.

"This is a six-pack," he sneered, then poked Wilko's stomach. "This is from too many six-packs."

He grinned unpleasantly as he loomed over the smaller Tasmanian. Suddenly there was a loud crack. The policeman's eyes lost focus as he crumpled to the floor.

"And this was one single bottle," observed Jazz, standing behind Steinmetz and brandishing the now broken weapon she'd picked up from a desk.

Wilko shook his head as he said, "I was brought up to respect the police. I don't have anything like the history John has with them. Hobart didn't have issues with protests and street marches and corruption – not in my experience anyway. But lately I just seem to keep seeing the worst of them."

"Yes, I'm sure you're really just misunderstood," said a quiet unexpected voice from behind them. Sergeant Conroy stood very still, framed by the rear doorway of the station office. Wilko and Jazz looked extremely uncomfortable.

"I saw what you did to my constable," continued Conroy, his voice still low. "And I saw and heard why. I'm not surprised that he's done no paperwork to explain why you're in custody."

Jazz tried a smile. "Good help's hard to find, eh?"

"Don't be smart, young lady. You don't know the half of it. I'm afraid sometimes some of my blokes do more harm than good. But that doesn't mean I can just turn a blind eye when you bust a bottle over the head of one of them."

"Ah – well…" Wilko groped for something to say.

Jazz was quicker. "Self-defence! We were provoked!" she exclaimed.

Conroy nodded slowly. "Mm. Yeah, I can see there is something in that." He stroked the stubble on his chin as he considered. Walking into the room he stepped over Steinmetz's prone form and sat on the edge of a desk.

He looked thoughtfully at the two companions. "This bloke who laid the initial allegation against you, Drayden – I met him and I have to admit I wasn't real impressed. From some of his story and what I just overheard do I get the impression he's a friend of yours?"

Wilko snorted. "Used to be. I thought so, anyway."

The sergeant nodded. "I reckon one of the great tragedies of the human race is that people change." He looked down at Steinmetz before continuing, "Of course, that also is one of mankind's greatest hopes, too. So – why did this Drayden character drop you in it? Just his idea of fun? I know that type."

Jazz scowled. "I think he's trying to stop us from finding Harlan. My boyfriend."

"Finding him?" responded Conroy mildly.

"He's an archaeologist. He's supposed to have been working with Drayden and another chap but they're denying ever seeing him. But I heard from him just before he arrived here and I'm sure they're covering something up!"

"So – we've got a missing person report on your boyfriend?" asked the sergeant.

Wilko and Jazz looked at each other. Their embarrassment was clear on their faces.

"Y'know, that might have been a good idea," said Wilko sheepishly.

Sergeant Conroy sighed quietly. "Yep. Might have been. Pull up a couple of chairs. I'll put Steinmetz on a bunk in a cell to sleep off his headache, and then you two can tell me your story."

.o0o.

Scarlet and Darren sat on the edges of their respective beds in 'her' room. On their laps were plates on which breakfast had been served.

They had received what was the typical Murph's Mob breakfast, regardless of whose turn it might have been to cook – fat sausages swimming in grease like pigs in a deep wallow. All that varied according to whoever cooked was the depth of the grease. Darren had managed most of one sausage. Scarlet had looked at the contents of her plate in some kind of horror, and had watched in morbid fascination as the whole mess slowly congealed.

"I'm sure this counts as cruel and unusual treatment," she said.

Darren grinned. "Not unusual for these guys I reckon. I think the Surfie's actually trying to do the right thing by us, as best he knows."

Scarlet shook her plate gently. The contents didn't even wobble any more. "If this is his best, I'd hate to imagine his worst. Wait - 'Surfie' you said?"

"Just Murph's name. Makes me think of Murphy The Surfie. He was a professional wrestler on TV back in the early seventies. I've always loved the name."

Scarlet blinked. "The early seventies? That was before you were born! How do you know about him?"

"You know about things from before you were born, don't you?" replied Darren with some irritation.

"I do a lot of research."

"Well, John tells me about old wrestlers and boxers when we're watching matches on the telly."

Scarlet shook her head and looked away. "There's so much he should be blamed for…"

"It's popular culture! Stop being a snob!"

The colouring that helped provide her nickname flared. "I am not a snob!" She paused. "Am I? I don't mean to be."

"Well, it happens."

"I'm truly sorry – I will try not to let it. But – wrestling? Boxing?"

Darren grinned. "Oh, I've never gotten into them as much as John. I think they're a bit of a release for him. I think he used to fight, but until… recently, I've never seen him actually hit anyone. I think he might be worried he'd… I don't know - enjoy it somehow."

They both were silent for a moment, remembering recent incidents that had prompted John B. to violence. He certainly hadn't taken any backward steps.

Scarlet looked at Darren with new respect in her eyes. "You do care about him a lot, don't you?"

"We've been mates for years – since I was a kid and he was just about the only person who treated me seriously. He's my best friend. I know he'd look out for me if I needed him. He's done it before. That's why I'm here on this trip." There was a long pause before he asked "What about you? Why did you come along?"

"I came to that evil place in the desert because I feel it's my responsibility to use my knowledge to combat the Forces of Darkness."

"Wow – really? You do that a lot?"

"Well, I must admit I hadn't had what you might call a real opportunity before. I think – I hope – threats like that don't come along too often."

Darren nodded. "Yeah, you'd hope not! Pretty brave of you to tackle it, then."

"Brave?" Scarlet replied, blushing again. "Oh, well… I don't know. I felt… responsible…"

"Yeah? How come?"

"Oh , ah, I…" The blush subtly changed colour. It never had become quite clear to anyone else just how Scarlet's actions had involved them in the bizarre plot under the military base. Although it turned out to be a good thing they were, she was still a little reticent about explaining how she'd managed to put their lives at risk.

She composed herself a little. "Nothing. I… er, felt that my research meant I had a responsibility to be involved. I knew – or at least had a strong suspicion as to what was going on there."

Darren looked like he was about to ask another uncomfortable question, and Scarlet was momentarily relieved when there was a loud knock on the door.

"It's me, Murph. I'm comin' in. Hope you're decent, Red. Hey, with Skinny in there too you better be!"

Darren only grinned but Scarlet looked thoroughly flustered when the biker boss walked in, closely followed by Burg, Geezer, Curls and Pretty Boy.

Murph turned to his mates and said, "Ah, guys – it's a bit crowded in here. Wait outside, eh? I can talk to these two without backup."

With only a little grumbling the four complied.

"Breakfast okay?" the 'boss' asked genially.

Darren answered before Scarlet could say anything undiplomatic. "Not much appetite till we know what's going on."

"Fair enough." He grinned his gap-toothed grin. "Don't reckon it was quite to your taste anyway, eh Red? We still got no word from our 'good mate' Carl Costelow. I'm startin' to wonder if he was setting us up after all. But why would he bother?"

"Costelow? He's the one who wanted you to keep us locked up? That's the bloke that was shouting in the park the other day isn't it? The lawyer. Wilko and Jazz were supposed to be seeing him yesterday," said Darren.

Scarlet nodded her agreement. "It's all too much of a coincidence, isn't it? I think it's got something to do with whatever's going on at Cobbemarmoo."

Seeing the puzzled look on Murph's face, the two reluctant 'guests' gave a hurried explanation of their search for Harlan Hunter, or at least news of him. Their only clue had been the mysterious place name: Cobbemarmoo.

"It's up in the ranges. Out of the way spot. Lots of rocks and a bad reputation that goes back a long way. No one goes there," explained the biker.

"But you know the way to Cobbemarmoo?" asked Scarlet, unthinkingly grabbing his hand.

Murph made no attempt to remove her grasp as he answered, "Yeah, pretty well. Got family come from that way. Silly bloody lawyer should've just asked me about the place – I'd have told him there's nothin' good to find there."

"Hopefully we'll find Jazz's boyfriend there. That at least would be good!" corrected Scarlet.

Darren gave a wry smile. "Wilko might not agree a hundred percent."

The redhead looked at him in surprise, and then gave another quiet little exclamation as she realized she was still holding Murph's hand.

The black man gave her fingers a gentle playful squeeze before separating their clasp.

Disconcerted on two fronts, Scarlet struggled for words. "I don't think

Robert would…"

"Wilko wouldn't wish harm on anybody, I reckon. That's not what I meant. I think he's taken a bit of a fancy to Jazz himself, that's all."

"Really? I thought John… Well. Really? You know, I think I don't understand people very well."

"Nobody understands the 'sweet mystery of romance' I reckon," grinned Murphy, giving her a wink as he left the room, leaving the breakfasts to set solidly on their plates at the end of Darren's bed.

Murph called out as he walked back into the lounge, "Burg, Curls, Geezer – with me. Don't worry Red, we'll get you there. Skinny, I guess you'll be coming too?"

As he and Scarlet left the room Darren met Murph's look and answered, "You want to try to stop me?"

The gang leader grinned. "Nope! Reckon you're entitled to one o' these."

He pulled a leather jacket, emblazoned with the grinning gap-toothed skull from a coat hook and tossed it to the young man. "You fight like one of us, you comin' out on a job with us, you can look like one of us. Come on. We'll take the Beast," he shouted as he broke into a run and dashed out the back door.

The jacket was probably two sizes too large for Darren, but the way his wiry frame swelled with pride as he hurriedly pulled his new colours on –

well, it would have to be a brave, or foolhardy, bloke who'd tell him so.

To the considerable surprise, and relief, of Scarlet (and probably Darren), the Beast turned out to be a large, long-wheel-based, air-conditioned four wheel drive wagon. It was fitted out to comfortably seat nine people. The Beast sat parked in its own carport alongside the collection of motorcycles that would more usually be expected of Murph's Mob.

Darren, Curls and Geezer clambered into the back of the vehicle, carrying a small assortment of weaponry.

Now seated in the middle of the front bench seat, flanked by Burg and the driver Murph, Scarlet looked about and blinked. "Well, this is – a surprise," she said uncertainly.

Murph grinned. "What d'you think we are – savages?"

"No, no! Of course not! I just… er…" she tried to reply, shifting uncomfortably.

"It's okay," said the Mob's leader, his grin broadening even further. He reached down and gave Scarlet's leg a playful squeeze. "Just havin' a go at you."

To her own surprise, she made no move to shift his hand.

Burg was still trying to catch up with what was going on. "Ain't we waiting for Mr. Costelow to call, boss?"

"No, mate," replied his boss. "There's somethin' screwy goin' on and I reckon our friend Carl's in it right up to his ginger eyebrows."

212

"But you said we should trust Mr. Costelow," the big man persisted.

"That was in the courtroom mate, when that…" Murph looked sideways at Scarlet and chose his language carefully. "When Steinmetz was tryin' to fit you up. When it was Costelow's job to be on our side."

Geezer spoke up uncertainly. "Costelow knows a lot of stuff."

Murph grinned. "Mate, I know a lot of stuff. So does Red, I reckon. So do you, when it comes right down to it. Carl knows a lot about the law. That ain't the same thing as bein' honest."

"So why do you work for him?" asked Darren. There was no sarcasm or malice in the question, just open curiosity.

The boss' grin faded. "We don't, okay Skinny? We do him a favour here and there, like lookin' after you guys or bein' around an' makin' the right sort of noises when he's doin' his political thing. He looks after us when any of the Mob gets in strife and winds up in court. Let's face it mate, even out here a lotta folks look twice at the likes of us. Some folks 'cos of the bikes, some folks 'cos of the colours, and some folks – well, some folks just don't like a bunch of blokes hangin' around together."

Darren nodded. "Yeah. Sorry mate, no offence meant. A lot of people look at things without really seeing them."

Scarlet chewed the inside of her lip for a moment. Was that directed at her? Probably not deliberately, she realised, but in recent days she'd found herself reconsidering a lot of things that had been taken for granted for a while. Things about other people, and things about herself.

If Murph was aware of her introspection he gave no sign of it. He replied to Darren, "No worries mate. No offence taken. Yer dead right about people and how they look at things."

"Yeah," agreed Curls, not noted as the deepest of thinkers. "Some people oughta have a bloody good look at 'emselves before they have a go at anyone else."

*

The white police wagon bounced and pitched along what might be generously called the road. The surface deteriorated the further from Alice Springs that they travelled.

"You sure you know the way to this Cobbemarmoo place?" Wilko asked Conroy.

"A way, probably not the way," replied the policeman. "Round here it's not so much knowing roads as directions and landmarks, and finding your way between 'em. I may not be an actual local, but I've been out here for a while and it pays a good copper to get to know the lay of the land."

"And I reckon you're a good copper," observed the Tasmanian. "You're restoring my faith in the force a bit, anyway."

The sergeant grinned, even as he concentrated on holding the wagon on the sliding sandy surface at speed. "Thanks mate. Don't be too hard on Serge Steinmetz. It's a tough environment out here, and you've gotta be tough enough to deal with it."

"That doesn't mean you have to be a bully, or a thug. You're not," said Jazz.

"Thanks. Again. I'm a bit older than Serge though, and I've been out here a bit longer. I'll read the riot act to him when we get back, he'll grizzle, I'll tell him to pull his head in and hope he's learned a bit of a lesson. Look out – might be a bit of a squeeze between these rocks but I want a bit of height to look around from."

Conroy had managed to maneuver the wagon up through a tumble of rocks to a small plateau that offered a reasonable view along shallow valleys and over low outcrops. Shading his eyes with his hand he looked to the northwest.

"Did either of you see that?" he asked.

"See what?" replied Wilko.

"Something funny in the sky over there, just for a moment?" wondered Jazz.

Conroy nodded. "Almost like a flash of light, but not quite."

"It was almost like the sky – distorted in one spot."

Wilko peered in the direction the other two were indicating and shook his head. "Maybe I blinked. Sometimes I think I must look without seeing things."

As Conroy started to drive in the direction of the point he'd noticed, Jazz squeezed the Tasmanian's knee playfully.

"Don't sell yourself short," she said. "Oops! No offense intended!"

"None taken. Not from you."

The smiles exchanged belied the fact that they were on a mission to find Jazz's missing boyfriend – something that Sgt. Conroy noticed in his mirror but was smart enough not to comment on.

*

Navigation by cat, or rather by Kat, proved to be quite straightforward if perhaps baffling to anyone who didn't know the big Persian.

He sat quietly shedding fur onto Harlan's lap in the sidecar while John B. steered the Ariel between rocks and dunes. If the wizard headed in a direction Kat didn't agree with there would be a loud yowl. The bike would be slowed down or stopped until Kat, sniffing at the air, faced in a particular direction and gave a short mmreh.

"He's quite an animal," Harlan had observed approvingly.

"Smarter than the average," agreed John B. "Average cat, average animal, most average people I think. Certainly he keeps surprising me and we've been mates for quite a few years now."

At one point Harlan was disturbed when the cat let out a strange sort of growl, stood up, half climbed out of the sidecar and whipped his tail fiercely a few times before settling back down to his usual equanimity.

The archaeologist looked at the scratches made in the wooden shell of the sidecar where one paw had been resting and was silently glad no claws had been extended through his canvas trousers.

"I wonder what that was about?" the Hawaiian said.

Stewart shook his head. Reacting to the big Persian's behavior he'd slowed the bike down to just above stalling speed, but when Kat settled back down he accelerated again.

Thoughtfully the wizard replied, "Nothing good. I think we'll know soon enough."

.o0o.

Walter Bevan had finished preparing his second clearing. In the sand he'd scratched a complicated pattern of circles, triangles, odd shapes and wavy lines. The pattern may have looked vaguely familiar to Harlan, or to Scarlet, but neither would have recognized the details or the way they fitted together.

Not many people would, and most of them would have run away screaming if they really understood.

The professor had once more donned his academic gown, after again taking the time to review and check his memory of a long, difficult series of what, in the absence of a better term might be called phrases. A series of sounds and syllables, Bevan may not have pronounced them quite correctly. But there was nobody in a position to correct him even in the unlikely event he would accept correction. In this, more than anything in his entire life, he was absolutely certain that he was right.

Now he stood in the middle of one of the triangles he'd drawn – not in the middle of the pattern, but in the upper left quadrant. Sinister and superior, the man had mused to himself as he'd traced the lines in the sand. He began to recite.

After some moments he stopped, and drank a deep draught of the silver contents of the bowl he held.

He waited.

Yes. He felt the change. He was stronger. Already fading were the aches and pains of age – of humanity. He drank another mouthful, and rolled his shoulders, flexing muscles in his back. They were muscles that had been quite well developed in his youth on the farm, and that even recently could still wield a shovel effectively. But he knew as he stretched them under his robe that they had never felt so powerful.

The unexpected sound of an engine at high revs caused the professor to look around in considerable irritation. He frowned in puzzlement as a large four wheel drive skidded to a halt near the campsite.

As Murph switched off the motor he called to his Mob, "Boys, I want a word with that bugger."

Curls and Geezer were on the side of the vehicle nearest the archaeologist.

"We'll get 'im boss," called the bald biker as they jumped out and started to run towards Bevan.

"Don't you dare!" shouted Bevan. "None may touch Yam-nahar!" He gestured imperiously and a small powerful tornado immediately sprang up under the feet of the two bikers.

The hapless pair didn't have time to shout or even scream as the wind flung them into the air to land hundreds of metres away. They landed heavily and didn't move.

Scarlet looked shocked and grabbed Murph's arm as he went to leap from the Beast.

"I know that name! Yam-nahar. One of the dark gods!" she exclaimed.

Murph pulled free of her grip and got out of the truck. She dived after him. Burg had run around from the other side of the Beast with Darren trailing only by the moments it took to grab a weapon.

Bevan's eyes were wide and wild as he put the bowl on the ground. He shouted, "No! Not a dark god! A golden god!"

Arms outstretched he slapped his hands together. A fierce gale sprang up, lifting sand and blasting it at the four who were running towards him.

Murph spun and grabbed Scarlet. He threw her to the ground then flung himself on top of her to protect her from the scouring sands.

Burg battled forward against the increasing gale and bellowed, "I'll get 'im boss!"

The burly adjutant struggled on, his feet slipping in the soft surface. He held an arm in front of his face as some protection. The protection wouldn't last long, possibly neither would the arm – the leather of his jacket's sleeve was already shredding. His t-shirt was already in tatters and the sand was flaying the skin from his belly.

Murph shouted something but the words were lost in the howling wind. Suddenly Burg's legs buckled as a kendo stick struck the back of his left knee – a kendo stick with all of Darren's weight behind it. As the biker fell the young man dived onto the ground beside him and pulled his own newly won jacket over both their heads.

"What the - ?" Burg began.

Darren shouted in his ear, "Keep your head down! Murph doesn't want to lose his best man, does he?"

"Best man? Is Murph getting married?"

Darren rolled his eyes and tried to burrow into the earth while keeping an air pocket around them.

Another engine was just audible over the howling sandstorm. It was the police wagon, skidding into the professor's first clearing.

His attention focused on Murph's Mob, the professor didn't notice the new arrivals at first. So perplexed as they were at what was going on, they had the opportunity to jump from the vehicle in relative safety. Wilko almost jumped straight onto the remains of Carl Costelow.

"Hey – it's a mummy! What's it doing out here… wait a minute – this looks like that lawyer!"

Jazz and Conroy looked down at the pitiable ruin – the skin looked like old brown paper stretched over a skeleton.

"That's him alright," agreed the blonde, evidently unfazed by the grisly sight.

"Can't say as I'll miss him, but someone's going to have to answer for this," said the sergeant grimly.

Jazz snorted and pointed towards the black-robed figure in the other clearing. "Looks pretty clear who's your prime suspect, but bugger him – where is Harlan?"

She shouted at Bevan, "You evil old coot – where's my boyfriend?"

Eyes afire after another mouthful of the silver essence, the professor didn't even bother to answer her. He slammed his hands together again to generate another gale, this time directed at the policeman and the two companions.

"Back behind the van!" shouted Conroy.

Jazz paused briefly, still trying to face down the figure in the black robe, but the force of the wind and the impact of the sand forced her to turn to follow the sergeant's advice. With the gale behind her she was almost blown past the wagon but Wilko reached out and grabbed her arm. Gripping the wheel arch with his other hand he hauled her in to join him kneeling in the lee of the back of the van.

"Where the hell did this sandstorm come from?" yelled the Tasmanian.

The sergeant didn't answer. He turned and braced his back against the side of the vehicle, digging his feet into the sand as best he could and locking his legs. He gestured for the others to do the same as the wagon started to give signs of lifting off the ground.

'If this thing flips on us we're stuffed!' he realised, but couldn't think of a solution.

Had Conroy known it, the hope of a solution was approaching from another direction.

John B., Kat and Harlan had spotted Curls and Geezer, and although they didn't recognize them had stopped to check on the two blokes. It was due entirely to luck and not care on the professor's part that they had landed on sand and not rock. That would have been fatal. As it was, both were bruised and breathless. Gasping with the impact and shock, holding what felt like cracked ribs, the bald biker had at least been conscious. His younger mate was out cold, but was at least still breathing.

Curls waved away the offer of help and gestured toward the campsite. "Some old guy… crazy… just bloody pointed at us, weird bloody wind came outta nowhere… threw us both like bloody toys…"

Stewart and Hunter exchanged looks.

"Sounds like we're too late," said the Hawaiian.

"Never too late while we're breathing, mate. I just wish we had a clue about what we should do, though," answered the wizard.

"*Rraow!*" was Kat's contribution.

"Onward it is, then," said John B. "We'll be back as soon as we can, mate," he said to Curls.

The biker nodded his tattooed head. "Make sure… the others are okay," he panted.

"Others?"

"Murph 'n' Burg. Skinny 'n' Red, too…" he replied as closed his eyes and gritted his teeth.

Stewart revved the motorcycle and pulled away. 'Skinny and Red? Is that who I think it is, I wonder?' he mused.

They arrived at the edge of the clearing, directly behind Bevan and seemingly out of his line of sight. The Ariel's motor was too quiet to be heard over the sound of the windstorm. John B. momentarily considered accelerating and ramming into the professor but stopped the bike when suddenly the black-robed figure turned and faced them.

"Yam-nahar senses a new challenge! Now who dares…?" Bevan's voice trailed away and his eyes widened as he recognized Harlan Hunter.

The gales whipping at the bikers, the policeman and the companions died down as abruptly as it had appeared.

"You? You are supposed to be dead!" roared the figure inside the clearing.

John B. gave a wry grin and said, "Well, you got that wrong for a start."

Tendrils of energy like golden fire crackled around the black robe.

"I… Yam-nahar is never to be corrected! The situation is quickly remedied! You will die, American!"

Jazz looked out around the back of the police van, Wilko still restraining her from running out into Bevan's view. "Harlan!" she called.

The Hawaiian waved at her in recognition, but addressed the professor. "Of course I'll die. Everyone does. I really don't think you should be doing this, sir."

"Do not presume to lecture to Yam-nahar! You are as nothing to me. I am a god! When I have consumed the last of this elixir I will be the god made manifest, and my first act will be to destroy all of you, utterly!"

Scarlet held Murph and said fearfully, "I don't know how to stop him!"

Murph's body was tense but he replied, "Why would you reckon you should know, Red? Me, I dunno what to stop, far less how!"

Burg turned to Darren and asked through a mouthful of sand, "How quick you reckon we can get to him, Skinny?"

The young man looked up over the edge of the small depression they'd managed to create for themselves. "Nothing like quick enough, mate," was his reluctant and similarly stifled answer.

Jazz turned to Conroy. "Haven't you got a gun?" she demanded.

"He can't shoot an unarmed man, can he?" asked Wilko.

"Not sure about 'unarmed' – I'm not even sure about 'man' now. I think he just looks like one. And he wants to kill Harlan!" was her reply.

Conroy shook his head and said, "Folks, I'm not sure about any of this. He's threatened to kill all of us, though, so while you might not have noticed I did actually try to bring him down." He held up the gun that Jazz hadn't seen on the other side of his body. "Dunno what happened to the bullets. If they hit him he didn't even notice."

Harlan climbed from the sidecar as John B. stepped off the Ariel.

225

With surprising calm Stewart remarked, "To borrow an old expression, this bloke's full of wind and water like the barber's cat – no offence, little mate."

Harlan forced himself to be similarly calm, presuming (incorrectly) that John B. was trying to needle the professor as part of a cunning plan. "That's an interesting expression," he said.

"Goes back a long way. Wind and water… wind and water… Didn't you say the carvings you read here had something to do with 'mastering the elements'? Elements like, say, this wind?"

"That's right. Not much water round here though," the Hawaiian pointed out.

"Seems he can do plenty of damage with the wind, anyway," admitted the wizard.

"You will shortly see the damage Yam-nahar can do!" shouted the thing shaped like Walter Bevan as it raised the bowl to consume the last of the silver liquid.

Both men squared their shoulders and prepared to charge forward, admittedly with no idea of what they might achieve.

Kat walked past them both and sat very deliberately in front of them, staring at the robed figure. The big Persian's tail flicked rapidly, but he was otherwise still, apparently transfixed by the lines of golden light swirling around the professor.

John B. grabbed Harlan's shoulder. "Wait!" he cried. "All of you – hold still!" he shouted at the other two groups at different parts of the edge of the clearing

"But…" Scarlet began.

"Who's he? The cavalry?" asked Murph, interrupting quietly.

"I hope so!" was her equally quiet reply.

John B. pointed to the cat. "Watch Kat. Trust him!"

"Are you…?

Whatever Harlan had been about to ask John B. was lost. As the professor swallowed the last of the elixir his figure disappeared inside a rapidly expanding bubble of golden light. With the light came a hurricane wind, blowing out in all directions at once from the central point of where Bevan had been standing.

The archaeologists' campsite was flattened. Humans and cat flattened themselves to the ground as wind, sand and the energy wave that was visible as light passed over them. The withered husk of Carl Costelow was torn to fragments that were flung up and away like the dry leaves that they resembled. The Ariel skidded sideways for several yards. The doors and panels of the two wagons were pushed in.

The roar of the wind died away, not abruptly but quickly. Everyone looked up as best they could from under a layer of sand.

Where Bevan had stood was now an enormous fish, something like a carp with gleaming golden scales. Eyes the size of cart wheels whirled madly. Teeth like rows of cutlasses snapped.

It lay on its belly, broad tail thrashing up sand, the great head twisting frantically from side to side.

Even Kat ducked his head down to avoid the flail and the damage it could cause.

.o0o.

The great fish tried to breath but there was no life giving water – only red dust to clogs its gills. As it frantically tried to suck air the massive glittering body thrashed and flailed, the broad flat paddles of the tail and fins slapping the ground raising more clouds of the choking sands. All it could achieve was the hastening of its own demise.

It's often said that the eyes are the windows of the soul. There was no trace of the soul of Walter Bevan visible in the great portholes of Yam-nahar's head. There was no trace of anything human.

The huge round eyes began to cloud over as the convulsions weakened. Soon it could barely twitch.

Kat calmly padded over to the gigantic golden form, following his nose. He levered up a saucer-sized scale with one paw and tried an experimental bite of the fishy flesh below. Evidently it was an acceptable taste, as he began to do the same with another scale.

"Should we be letting him do that, do you think?" wondered Harlan aloud.

John B. dusted sand from his purple t-shirt then shoved his hands nonchalantly into the pockets of his jeans. "I wouldn't be the one to try to stop him. Get between Kat and food? Not wise. I think he's pretty sharp about what he will and won't eat, anyway."

The Hawaiian nodded in understanding. Suddenly Kat took a quick step back from his supersized snack, his tail erect and quivering.

With an irritated "*Mmreh!*" he bounded back towards the wizard, who had already taken a couple of concerned steps towards him.

A hazy glow emanated from the huge golden form. The haze thickened and became a glittering fog that enveloped the whole fish. Then with a sound like a soft sigh it dissipated falling to the ground as a shower of sand, lighter in hue than the surrounding red earth.

The god of the ancient mariners was gone. Just visible among the golden sand was the body of Walter Bevan – less desiccated than the withered remains of Carl Costelow, but just as clearly leached of water. Although the corpse lay on its belly, the back was arched and so severely twisted that Bevan's face looked up to the sky. In the dried out face the mouth was open in a final, permanent O.

Gradually everyone got to their feet, and made tentative steps toward the centre of the clearing.

Wilko looked at the late professor and shuddered. "I've got to try to stop doing that goldfish thing I get accused of. It's really not a good look. But where the hell did the giant fish that fell on the old bloke come from? I mean, I've heard of showers of fish falling from the sky during storms, but they're supposed to be small, and that's supposed to be rare, and… this thing was enormous… and… there was no storm… except maybe a sandstorm?" His voice trailed off weakly.

Conroy patted Wilko's shoulder sympathetically. "I don't wonder at anything I see out here, mate," he said.

Wilko looked at him with raised eyebrows. "You mean you understand what just went on?"

"Nope. Just don't wonder at it. Safer and easier that way."

The Tasmanian nodded. "I should try that."

"Yep. You should do, but I don't reckon you're the type. You worry too much."

Wilko sighed. "I hear that a lot. I reckon I've a right to. It's the company I keep…" he mused as he watched John B. He turned back to the sergeant and asked, "How are you going to write this up?"

Conroy considered for a moment then replied, "Acting on information received, I arrived at the campsite to find Mr. Costelow already deceased, apparently the result of dehydration. Soon after I determined that Professor Bevan had also expired. Cause of death… hmmm… overexposure and heatstroke."

"No questions asked?"

"Are you asking any?"

Wilko looked around the campsite. He watched familiar and unfamiliar figures trying to remove the red dust from themselves, and in some cases each other. Most of the excavation and the encampment itself were lost under a covering of sand, to which a wafting breeze was already adding a new layer.

"Best not to, eh?" observed the smaller man.

"That's the way," agreed the policeman cheerily.

John B. walked over to join them.

"There are a couple of blokes a bit the worse for wear over that way a bit. Breathing, but only one of them's conscious. They got picked up and dumped by a big wind, the bald one reckoned – that fits with everything we just saw. They're some of Murph's Mob by the look of them. I'll navigate if you want to go pick 'em up and check on them," he offered.

The policeman nodded. "Sounds like I'd better. Hang on." He strode over to the biker boss.

"Murph," he greeted.

"Sarge," was the reply. There was cautious respect in each voice – two men who knew and understood each other's positions.

"Couple of your blokes found over that way a bit. Knocked around but alive. I'm going to go collect them."

"We take care of our own, Sarge."

"You got any first aid training?" asked the policeman.

"No," admitted Murph.

Scarlet rested her hand on his shoulder and said, "Let the man do his job. You'll bring them straight back here before you go into town, won't you?" It was clear she would accept only one answer from Conroy.

"Yeah, alright – er – ma'am," replied the sergeant, slightly disconcerted by having both himself and Murph ordered about so casually.

As he climbed into the police van he addressed Stewart who was already in the passenger seat with Kat on his lap. "She's a handful, I reckon," he said as they drove towards where Geezer and Curls lay.

"Really? She's never been noted for it. Amazing what a change of environment can do, eh?"

The Persian gave a casual mmreh.

"Yep," agreed John B. "Yam-nahar just found that out the hard way."

"Who?" asked Conroy, already bemused by the cat's apparent contribution to the conversation.

"The big fish. A god of some of the old Mediterranean races – one of the more senior, nastier ones according to Harlan."

"Harlan? That would be the American bloke nobody thought to lodge a Missing Person report about?"

"Um… yeah, that's the one. Found him. Sorry, it didn't occur to me to drop into the station, I'm afraid. I haven't had a lot of positive experience with your… colleagues, around the country."

Conroy nodded as he drove. "I got that impression from your Tasmanian mate. I can't help your past I'm afraid. Best I can do is point out that, like every other job, we're not all the same."

"Good to hear. I'll keep it in mind. Left around this dune. And…
thanks."

Back at the former excavation site, Burg ambled over to where Scarlet
was now carefully brushing sand from Murph's face.

"Um, boss, what's this about you getting married?" he said nervously.

Scarlet and Murph both spun to face him and simultaneously exclaimed,
"What?!?"

"Well, Skinny said I was gonna be your best man…"

Wilko and Darren had walked over behind the big man.

"What's all this?" asked the Tasmanian.

With a hand over his eyes Darren explained, "Aw geez, when I was
trying to get Burg to keep his head down out of the sandstorm I told him
Murph wouldn't want to lose his best man."

Scarlet blushed while she sighed with some relief as Murph laughed out
loud and said, "You're right enough there!"

Wilko shook his head, more than a little puzzled by the interactions
between Darren, Scarlet and the bikers. He determinedly was not looking
across the clearing.

Across the clearing Jazz and Harlan shared a long hug.
"Sorry to have worried you, dear," said the archaeologist quietly. "I'd
have contacted you if I could."

They broke their embrace as the blonde said quietly, "I know, it's okay. I got well looked after."

"They seem like a good bunch of people," smiled Harlan.

"They are," agreed Jazz. "Hey, come on over here!" she called to Wilko.

The Tasmanian looked a little uncomfortable. "It's okay – I'm, er, talking to these guys. Thought I should give you two some space," he replied.

The Hawaiian waved airily. "It's alright, isn't it dear?"

"Of course it is," she replied. "Never mind – we'll come to you."

Wilko was not a little discomfited when she took his hand while still holding Harlan's in her other hand. The archaeologist seemed unconcerned. Introductions were exchanged all round.

"This has been the weirdest 'vacation' on record," said Wilko. "I think I'm almost looking forward to the peace and quiet of the office. When John gets back we should work out when to head home."

Scarlet looked troubled. "Robert… I'm not coming with you. Please tell Ron when you get back."

"Tell him? Tell him what?"

The redhead blushed intensely. "Well… I…"

Her search for words was interrupted by the return of the police van, and the collective rush to check on Geezer and Curls. They were sitting up in the back seat, both awake but wincing with pain.

"Got a bit busted up, sorry boss," said the young biker ruefully.

Murph patted him on the shoulder, which elicited another wince of pain.

"Nothin' to apologise for, mate. Nothin' you coulda done," said the boss, sympathetically.

"Reckon not," Geezer agreed. "What happened while we was out of it?"

"Ah," said Murph, "I reckon that's a bit complicated…"

"We'll explain later," interjected Scarlet.

Wilko raised his hand, looking a little like a boy in class. "Um, Scarlet… just what are you wanting me to tell Kaiser Ron? And whatever it is, can't John do it?"

Stewart looked puzzled. "Do what? Have I missed something?"

"Quite a lot, really," replied Darren with a grin.

Scarlet squared her shoulders, her blush surprisingly having faded and not returned. "Robert, I'd like you to speak to Ron because, frankly, I think he takes you more seriously than John. No offense intended, John."

"None taken, fair comment," John B. conceded.

Scarlet continued, "I've decided to stay on here for a while. I've felt more – alive here than I can ever remember and I want to explore that."

"You thinkin' of stayin' with us, Red?" asked Murph, grinning. Curls and Geezer exchanged worried looks.

"Thank you for the offer, Murph."

"Actually, I'm not sure I…"

Scarlet interrupted the biker's mild protest, saying, "But I'd prefer to find a little place of my own for now, at least. I'm sure the sergeant could recommend somewhere if you can't. I would like you and I to stay in touch, though." She emphasized the word 'touch' by squeezing Murph's hand.

The biker boss nodded. "Fair enough, Red. Reckon I'd like that. What about you, Skinny? You're welcome to stick around with us if you want."

Burg, Curls and Geezer looked considerably happier with that suggestion.

Darren though, shook his head. "Thanks mate. I appreciate the offer. I'll come back into town in the Beast with you to make sure the guys are okay, but I'm only just starting to work out what I want to do with my life. For now, I reckon there's a few more options for me down south."

"Whatever ya reckon, mate. There's a place here for you any time you decide you wanna come back. You keep them colours though Skinny – you earned 'em," answered Murph.

John B. scratched his head. "Red? Skinny? I really have missed a bit, haven't I? Somebody fill me in when we get back into town, eh?"

"Do you want a lift back into Alice?" asked Conroy.

John B. shook his head. "You'll have a full enough car with Wilko, Jazz and Harlan."

The wizard looked across at those three, watching Jazz release the hands of both men to sit in the front passenger seat. He raised a quizzical eyebrow briefly, wondering what the future might hold there. "I just wish them all to be content with whatever works out between them," he said quietly to himself.

He turned back to the sergeant and continued, "I appreciate the offer, but I've still got the Ariel. I'll ride back, put Kat in the sidecar again. I'll leave the bike at your station for Old Black Guy to collect if you don't mind."

"Old Black…? Oh – right! Yeah, reckon I know the bloke you mean. He owns the bike, does he?"

"I'm not quite sure about the word 'owns', but he looks after it. I reckon you won't even need to get in touch with him - he'll just know where to find it."

The policeman looked thoughtful, then nodded. The character John B. named as 'Old Black Guy' had been around Alice Springs a lot longer than Conroy himself had been. There was an impression that he'd been around for as long as anyone could remember – he was just sort of there. Seemed a nice enough old bloke, and he just might be doing quite a bit 'behind the scenes' that made the job of policing a little bit easier.

"Fair enough. That wouldn't surprise me either," agreed the sergeant. "You heading back south after that?"

"Pretty soon," agreed Stewart with a smile. "There's a doctor in town I'd like to catch up with again before we go."

"Margaret Jones?"

"Yeah, that's the one. I said I'd try to see her again before I left."

"Bloody good woman that," observed the sergeant.

John B. didn't miss the defensive note in the policeman's voice. 'Message received and understood' he thought.

"You're right," the wizard agreed, climbing onto the Ariel and starting the motor. "Tell you what – I'll leave it to you to give her my regards – no, make it my good wishes. Let her know the hand is healing up well now. She'll know what that's all about." He met the gaze of Sgt. Conroy and continued, "And I'm glad she's got you to look out for her."

Conroy shifted a little uncomfortably and said, "Yeah, well, I do the best I can…"

Kat jumped into his compartment, ready to sleep. The wizard waved his hand in a kind of salute and smiled at the sergeant as he said, "That's all anyone can ask of anyone, mate. And all they should ask of themselves."

.o0XX0o.

-PATI-

Next: A secret laboratory on a small island in Bass Strait. Secrets

revealed, lives threatened…

THE MAD MACHINES OF MUNDARA

The Third Book of Dubious Magic